TWO WORLDS, ONE FAMILY

EDGE OF THE WORLD SERIES : BOOK 3

LEROY A. PETERS

PROLOGUE

Summer of 1835
Montgomery County, Maryland

The last fifteen years had not been too easy for the Hancock family. Four years previously, the patriarch of the family, Rev. Nehemiah Hancock, a staunch abolitionist, lost his church. It was burnt to the ground by his angry neighbors as a result of Nat Turner's Rebellion that took place in Jerusalem, Virginia that fall. The rebellion was led by a slave preacher named Nat Turner who, along with his men, killed sixty white men, women, and children, all of them from slave-owning families. It caused a massive response from many white slave owners up and down the South, and the result was over two hundred black Americans—both enslaved and free—were lynched and slaughtered up and down the Eastern seaboard from Maryland to Georgia. Most of them had nothing to do with the rebellion.

For Reverend Hancock and his wife, Abigail, it was personal, even before the rebellion. Being an abolitionist family, they were not very popular in Maryland. In March of 1820, their fourteen-year-old daughter, also named Abigail, was brutally raped by the son of the sheriff, who hated them. Their son Azariah, Abigail's twin brother, took justice into his own hands and killed her rapist. Knowing full well that he was as good as dead if he stayed, Azariah fled Maryland.

It got worse after that. Not long after her brother left, young Abigail found out that she was pregnant with her rapist's baby. Despite her young age, she decided to keep the child, and her parents supported her. In December of that year, she gave birth to her son, Caleb Nehemiah Hancock. Not long before her father lost the church when Caleb was seven, Abigail married Jason Allen, a close friend of her family. Their fathers both served in the War of 1812 together. Despite that Jason's family were slave owners, they were the Hancocks' closest friends.

Jason would adopt Caleb and raise him as his own, while he and Abigail had two sons of their own, Abraham and Jacob. After the church was burnt down, Jason's parents, John and Alice, invited Nehemiah and Abigail to live with them. Since then, Reverend Hancock continued to preach against the practice of slavery and would even preach to the slaves on the Allen plantation about freedom.

This day was no exception when a distinguished gentleman came to visit. John Allen Sr. and his wife, Alice, were having dinner with their family and the Hancocks when Moses, one of the house servants, came in and announced the visitor.

"Massa and Missus Allen," he said. "Mr. David Crockett is here to see Reverend and Missus Hancock."

Both Nehemiah and Abigail raised their heads in surprise, and they weren't the only ones.

"*The* Davy Crockett?" asked John Allen. "Coming here?"

"I prefer to be called David," said the distinguished former congressman from Tennessee as he walked in.

Everyone in the entire house stood there astonished, for David Crockett, the frontiersman and veteran of the War of 1812, a congressman only until recently, stood before them.

"Welcome to our home, Congressman Crockett," said Alice Allen.

"Please, just David will do, madam," said Crockett as he bowed before the lady of the house.

"What brings you to our home?" asked John.

"Do you have a Reverend Nehemiah and Abigail Hancock staying with you?"

Reverend Hancock, who was already standing from the dinner table, moved forward and introduced himself.

"Do you have a son named Azariah?" asked Crockett.

Both mother and daughter Abigail almost immediately shrieked as they suddenly stood beside the reverend as he nodded.

"How do you know?"

"About fifteen years ago," said Crockett, "before I entered politics, your son stayed with me and my family for a couple of weeks, before he went West." He pulled a letter from his coat and handed it to Reverend Hancock. "My wife and I received this letter last week," he said. "It is from your son."

Shaking nearly uncontrollably, Reverend Hancock took the letter and opened it.

"What does it say, Daddy?" asked a nervous Abigail.

"I am getting to that."

The reverend read the letter aloud:

Dear Loving Mother and Father,

It has been a long time. I pray all is well with you and Abigail. At the time of this writing, I have been living in the Rocky Mountains for the last fourteen years as a trapper and mountain man. With the help of my best friend and mentor, Liam O'Reilly, I have become not only good at trapping and making money but living in relative peace with many of the tribes and with the land.

God has blessed me not only with a good friend in Liam but also with a family, for I am married to an Indian woman named Sweet Grass. She is of the Arapaho Nation, and her people have adopted me as one of their own. Also, God has given us four healthy and beautiful children—Adam, Sara, and the twins, Abigail and Solomon. I wish you could meet them and my adopted tribe, as well as my in-laws. They have been great to me, and I wish I could share with you how beautiful the land and the mountains of the West are. I have missed you all.

How is sister Abigail? Please give her my love, and I pray that she has healed from her ordeal and she and Jason have gotten married. I know I can never return home, for that would mean my doom, but I wanted you to know that I am alive and well, and God has been good to me.

With love.

Your son,

Azariah Hancock

Had his wife and daughter not been standing on either side of him, Nehemiah would have collapsed. He gently sat down as he handed the letter to Mother Abigail, who by this time had tears of joy streaming down her cheeks. Sister Abigail was also crying with tears of joy as her husband, Jason, put his arms around her to comfort her.

"Who is Azariah, Ma?" asked five-year-old Jacob.

Jason turned to his youngest son and answered proudly for his wife, "He is your uncle, Jacob."

"How come we have never seen him?" asked six-year-old Abraham.

Everyone was quiet, including Caleb, who was going to be fifteen in December. Everyone, including David Crockett, knew the reason, but no one dared to say anything.

"A long time ago," Jason suddenly spoke, "your Uncle Azariah did a very brave and courageous thing. Unfortunately, many around here didn't see it that way, and he had to leave."

"Can he visit us?" asked Jacob.

"I'm afraid not, Jacob," answered Nehemiah.

Everyone could see the look of sadness on the reverend's face, a reflection shared by his wife and daughter.

"At least we know he is still alive," said Jason, who always had great admiration and respect for Azariah, especially after avenging Abigail's rape so many years ago. "Be proud of your brother, Abigail."

Abigail looked into the loving eyes of her husband as he continued to wipe away her tears. "I am," she said. "I just wish I could see him again and meet his wife and children."

"You're happy that your brother is married to a dirty Injun squaw?" snorted Maggie Allen.

Maggie was the wife of John Allen Jr. and not well-liked by the family. Neither Jason nor Abigail could stand her because she represented a typical stuck-up Southern socialite. Jason, as well as his parents, could not understand what John Jr. saw in her.

Maggie continued, "The fact he sired a litter of half-breeds, he should be ashamed of himself in my book!"

That was more than Mother Abigail was going to tolerate, and she responded by giving the pretentious Southern belle a right hook to the jaw, knocking her off her feet. "Those are my grandchildren you are talking about!"

Mother Abigail was about to do more damage before Caleb and Jason dragged her from Maggie, who was about to unleash her claws on the older lady, but her husband quickly grabbed her and put her over his shoulder and took her out of the room.

Abraham and Jacob were standing there dumbfounded at what their grandmother had just done, while John Sr. and Alice and the rest of the Allen family present were grinning from ear to ear.

Reverend Hancock immediately apologized to Congressman Crockett for his wife's behavior, but the former frontiersman just smiled and said, "You are a lucky man, Reverend. Your missus has spunk!"

Feeling that he had enough entertainment for one day, David Crockett bade farewell to both the Allen and Hancock families, who thanked him for delivering Azariah's letter. Knowing how much it meant to them, he informed both Reverend and Mrs. Hancock that their son was a grateful and an astounding young man when he was a guest in his home so long ago.

———————

Later that evening in their room, Nehemiah and Abigail read Azariah's letter again and again. It had been fifteen years since they last saw him. He would be twenty-nine years old now, the same age as his sister. How they both longed to have a chance to see him again. Suddenly there was a knock was on their door.

"Come in," said Nehemiah. It was Jason and Little Abigail.

"Everything okay in here?" asked Jason.

After both Nehemiah and Mother Abigail nodded, Jason gave his mother-in-law a smirk. "You have one hell of a right hook, Mother Abigail. Maggie will be lucky if she will be able to eat solid foods for a week."

"She had it coming," said Mother Abigail.

"What can we do for you both?" asked Nehemiah, wanting to change the subject.

"We just finished putting the boys to bed, and Jacob asked us an interesting question," said Jason.

"That being?"

"If Azariah cannot come and visit us, why can't we go and visit him?"

Both the reverend and Mother Abigail almost laughed until they realized that their son-in-law was not joking.

"Abigail and I have discussed it," Jason said. "There is nothing for us here, and it would be good for the boys to meet their uncle and cousins, especially Caleb."

Nehemiah turned to his daughter. "You sure about this, Abby?"

Little Abigail nodded. "I miss him, Daddy, and Jason is right. It would be good for the boys."

"Jason, what about your parents?" asked Mother Abigail.

"They'll understand," he said. "I think reuniting with my brother-in-law is more important, at least for my wife's sake."

Little Abigail turned to her husband and realized he meant every word of what he just said. He was doing this for her, her parents, and their sons.

"I know you want to be reunited with Azariah, also, and I don't think we should let anything short of the Almighty Himself keep that from happening."

Reverend and Mother Abigail looked at the letter again before making the only decision they could make. "When do we leave?"

1

MEMORIES

One year later, a few days out from the Green River.

Riding out of the Beartooth Mountains, two legendary trappers and their families were heading to Rendezvous, which was being held on the Green River. In the lead was the older of the two, Liam O'Reilly. At forty-six years of age, he had been in the Rocky Mountains since 1806, when he was just sixteen and a student of the legendary mountain man John Colter. Over the next thirty years, he had developed into a successful trapper extraordinaire. Known as Raging Bull by the tribes, the Irishman also had a fearsome reputation as someone you didn't mess with. His feud with the Crow was legendary after a

Crow war party murdered his first family. After avenging them, he earned his Indian name, and now just about every tribe of the Northern Plains and Rockies knew him as that.

Riding beside him was his best friend and pupil, Azariah Hancock. Known as He Who Walks Tall by the tribes, Azariah was also a legend in his own right, thanks to his mentor. Azariah was called He Who Walks Tall for two reasons. One was his immense height. At seven feet, five inches tall and weighing three hundred and fifty pounds, he was the tallest man in the West, among both white and red alike. The second reason was because he was known as a man of integrity and a man who had a reputation of killing rapists and other men of ill repute. Many of the tribes respected him for that, and most of his fellow trappers feared him for it.

Azariah first came out West sixteen years previously when he was just fourteen. Liam met Azariah in St. Louis that year and took him under his wing. Azariah was on the run from the law in Maryland for killing his twin sister's rapist.

For the past sixteen years, the two trappers were inseparable. Azariah looked at Liam as an older brother, and Liam looked at Azariah as a younger one. They both had red hair, though the Irishman was sixteen years older than Azariah and already had some gray. Azariah, now thirty, was of English-Scottish stock and wore his hair braided Indian-style in two plaits. Liam was nowhere near as tall as Azariah, but he was tall in his own right at six feet, four inches tall and weighed two hundred and fifty pounds. Both men had made a lot of money in the fur trade over the years—enough to live like kings in St. Louis—but neither felt they had any reason to ever return to civilization, no matter how much money they had.

Azariah turned his head to see one of the main reasons why he and Liam would never return to civilization, and he smiled. Riding behind them were two Indian women and some children.

Azariah was smiling at the younger of the two women, and she returned his smile. Her name was Sweet Grass, and she was of the Northern Arapaho Nation. For the last fifteen winters, she had been Azariah's wife and mother of their four children. Other than Liam, Azariah considered her his most trusted and best friend.

Riding on each side of her were their two youngest children, four-year-old twins Abigail Little Flower and Solomon White Wolf, who were watching the exchange between their parents.

Liam just shook his head as if embarrassed by the happy couple. "Will you two bloody knock it off!"

"What's in your craw, Liam?" asked Azariah.

"You and Sweet Grass acting like you are still newlyweds!"

The older Indian woman who was riding beside Sweet

Grass and the kids snorted in derision. "You are just as bad as they are, husband," she said.

The Irishman just rolled his eyes and sighed. "You're not helping, Choke Cherry Woman."

Choke Cherry Woman was of the Northern Cheyenne Nation, and for the past eight summers, she has been Liam's bride. She and her two daughters, Bluebird and Little Fawn, were kidnapped at the Rendezvous eight years previously by a band of Utes led by four white men. Liam and Azariah led a coalition of Arapaho and Cheyenne warriors to rescue them, and after they succeeded, she and Liam became close and eventually married later that summer. Since Choke Cherry Woman was a widow, Liam adopted her two daughters and raised them as his own.

Bluebird married a Cheyenne warrior named White Hawk and had given Choke Cherry Woman and Liam a grandson named Spotted Bear. Choke Cherry Woman and Liam also would have a child, a son named Luke Medicine Horse, who was seven and riding not far behind his mother and older sister, Little Fawn. Bluebird and her family lived among the Cheyenne and were waiting for them at Rendezvous.

Riding behind Azariah and Sweet Grass and helping to pull the pack train were their two eldest children, fourteen-year-old Adam Bear Claw and ten-year-old Sara Sunshine.

"What's a newlywed?" asked Solomon.

"A newlywed, son, is someone who just got married," answered Azariah.

"Why did Uncle Liam call you and Ma newlyweds?" asked Abigail.

"I said they *act* like newlyweds," said Liam. "Not that they were newlyweds."

"And what is so wrong with that?" asked Choke Cherry Woman with a twinkle in her eye. "We're worse than they are."

"Choke Cherry Woman!" shouted Liam. "Shush!"

Azariah, Sweet Grass, Choke Cherry Woman and the children laughed. "It's true, husband," said Choke Cherry Woman.

"But you don't have to let the whole bloody damn world know about it," derided Liam.

Azariah and Sweet Grass, along with Choke Cherry Woman, always enjoyed teasing Liam, grating on his nerves, but it was all in good fun. Liam always took life seriously, but he did have a sense of humor, more so than Azariah.

While the younger trapper could hold his own in jokes and teasing, he took life more seriously than his family and friends, though that didn't mean he didn't enjoy life. When he wasn't trapping for beaver, he preferred spending time with his family, especially his children. Both he and Sweet Grass were very young when they got married and started a family, but he took on the responsibility of husband and fatherhood head-on and without fail. Even though he never neglected his family responsibilities, he always gave most of the credit to Sweet Grass. She was a strong woman, both physically and mentally for a woman her age from the time she and the giant white man called He Who Walks Tall became husband and wife all that long ago. Sweet Grass and Azariah were not just husband and wife; they were a team.

While most marriages between trappers and Indian women during the fur trade were based on necessity, Azariah and Sweet Grass legitimately loved each other. Same for Liam and Choke Cherry Woman. Like his first marriage, Liam saw Choke Cherry Woman as an equal, and he loved her just as much as he loved his first wife Rain Cloud, who, along with their daughter, Constance, was taken from him by a Crow war party. A lot of white men took Indian women as their brides, but only did so for a season or two and then abandoned them before returning to civilization. It didn't matter if they had children with them or not. Liam and Azariah both looked down upon such men, mainly because marriage was for life, not for games to be played. Not to mention, children needed their fathers, as Liam and Azariah believed. Any man who abandoned their family was nothing more than a coward and not worthy of being called a man. Both men took their responsibilities as husbands and fathers very seriously and loved their wives and children very much. The thought of abandoning them for any reason never entered their minds. But that didn't mean their marriages were easy.

Interracial marriages were strongly frowned upon by

white people in the settlements east of the Mississippi River, but while it was tolerated and sometimes encouraged in the Rocky Mountains and the Plains during the fur trade didn't mean that those who partook in it didn't face their fair share of racism. Most whites hated mixed-blood Indian children in white society in the settlements, but they were also distrusted by some tribes as well.

Azariah and Sweet Grass, along with Liam and Choke Cherry Woman, had tried to protect their children from that kind of bigotry, especially at Rendezvous. While the Hancock children and Luke Medicine Horse had it better than most mixed-blood children, that didn't mean they were immune. One of the reasons white and red men respected the children was because they were afraid of their fathers. Liam and Azariah were respected among the trapping fraternity and the tribes because they were notoriously known for their bad tempers, Azariah especially. However, those tempers were triggered when some bigot, most likely a drunken trapper, disrespected their wives and children.

An incident occurred ten years prior at the 1826 Rendezvous. A drunken trapper made the mistake of calling Sweet Grass a squaw and demanded that Azariah hand her over to him and his friends. An enraged Azariah quickly threw a vicious right hook to the man's jaw, knocking him unconscious. What happened next is still talked about. Azariah pried open the unconscious man's jaws and then proceeded to rip out his tongue with his bare hands. Since then, at every Rendezvous, no one dared mess with or disrespect the wives and children of He Who Walks Tall and Raging Bull.

"Will Dr. Whitman be at Rendezvous again this year?" asked Sara.

"Who knows, Sunshine," answered Azariah.

Dr. Whitman was none other than Dr. Marcus Whitman, who, along with Rev. Samuel Parker appeared at the previous year's Rendezvous as missionaries to the Flathead and Nez Perce tribes. Azariah remembered how Dr. Whitman removed a Blackfoot arrowhead from the back of fellow mountain man Jim Bridger, after it had been stuck there for three years.

"I hope to see him again," said Sweet Grass. "I think he was a fascinating man."

"I don't trust him," said Choke Cherry Woman.

"You're not alone in that department, Choke Cherry Woman," said Azariah. "Don't get me wrong—I like him—but Christian missionaries coming out West to preach the faith to the tribes... I don't know about all that."

"Wasn't your father a holy man?" asked Little Fawn.

Azariah just shrugged. "He was a man of God, yes, but I don't think he considered himself a holy man."

"You rarely talk about him anymore, Pa," said Adam Bear Claw.

Azariah paused for a moment in thought. He admired how observant his eldest son was and thinking about it, he realized that Adam was right. He rarely thought about his family and often wondered if they were still alive after he was forced to leave them. "I have no reason to think about them, son."

"Why, Pa?"

Azariah realized that he not only had his son's undivided attention but the attention of all his kids and his wife as well. "I doubt that my parents are still alive after all these years; I mean, I hope they are, but my place is here with you and your mother."

Sweet Grass smiled at her husband's statement, but she knew he still thought of his parents and his twin sister, Abigail. While the nightmares about her predicament were long gone, she knew he never stopped thinking about her. She knew that her husband wished he could at least visit and see his family one more time.

2

1836 RENDEZVOUS

The day was July 6. This year's Rendezvous was getting started. The supply train led by Thomas Fitzpatrick had just arrived. Many of the trappers who relied on the supplies and who sold their plews to Fitzpatrick had been at the Green River since June 28. Among those accompanying the supply train was none other than Dr. Marcus Whitman and his party of missionaries. He brought his wife, Narcissa Whitman, and their colleagues Henry Spaulding and his wife, Eliza. It was the first time white women had come that far out West. They were a source of excitement and curiosity for both the trappers and the Indians who were at the Rendezvous. Most had never seen a white woman before. However, the missionaries weren't the only newcomers to the mountains.

Reverend Nehemiah Hancock and his family managed to convince Fitzpatrick to take them to the Rendezvous. After telling him who they were, Fitzpatrick didn't need much convincing. "Welcome to the Rendezvous, folks," he said.

Reverend Hancock and Abigail and their loved ones had a look of astonishment in their eyes as they stared at the multitude of trappers and Indian men, women, and children.

"Look at all the Indians, Ma!" exclaimed young Jacob.

"They are beautiful, aren't they, son?" said Little Abigail. "How are we going to find Azariah out here?"

"I'm sure Mr. Fitzpatrick can tell us which tribe he is staying with," said Reverend Hancock.

He was about to ask when a group of warriors and their wives approached the family. Most of them were staring at Mother and Little Abigail with curious eyes.

"Don't be afraid, ladies," said Fitzpatrick in his thick Irish brogue. "They have never seen white women before."

Taking that cue, the Hancock women extended their hands in friendship to the Indian women who accepted them. Reverend Hancock and Jason did the same to their husbands and the warriors spoke to them in a language that the newcomers couldn't understand.

"I'm sorry," said Jason. "But we don't speak your lingo."

"He asked if you are the white medicine men that have come to bring the white man's medicine to their people," said a trapper who had just approached the group.

Fitzpatrick had a smile on his face as he recognized the newcomer. "How the bloody hell are you, Bridger?"

Jim Bridger was well known among the tribes and the

trapping fraternity and had been in the trapping business for fourteen years. The thirty-two-year-old Virginian was part owner of the Rocky Mountain Fur Company until he and his partners sold it to their rivals, the American Fur Company, just two years prior.

"I am better now that I no longer have that damned Blackfoot arrow in my back," he said.

"What does your Indian friend mean by white man's medicine?" asked Reverend Hancock.

"There is no word for 'religion' in the Flathead tongue, which is the tribe my friend Digging Bear is from," answered Bridger. "They think you are missionaries and are with Dr. Whitman and his company."

"Oh," chuckled the reverend. "Kindly tell him no, we are not missionaries, but I thank him for the compliment."

Bridger laughed before translating the reverend's answer to Digging Bear. The Flathead warrior smiled and nodded that he understood before he and his group turned their attention to Dr. Whitman's group.

"I'm sorry, sir," said Bridger. "I didn't catch your name."

"Reverend Nehemiah Hancock," answered the reverend. "And this is my family."

Jim Bridger blinked. "You wouldn't happen to be related to an Azariah Hancock, now, would you?"

The reverend and his wife both smiled. "He is our son."

"Well, I'll be double-dog damned!" exclaimed Bridger. "I beg your pardon, Reverend," he then added quickly.

"I have heard worse, I assure you."

"Mr. Bridger, do you know where we could find our son?" asked Mother Abigail.

"Your best bet is among the Arapaho tribe and their allies, the Cheyenne," answered Bridger. "I don't keep company with the two tribes because they are enemies to my wife's people, the Flathead."

"Do you know where we can find them?" asked the reverend.

Bridger pointed south. "You will find the Cheyenne camped about a mile or two that way and the Arapaho camp farther west from them; however, be careful letting people know who you are."

"Why?" asked Mother Abigail.

Bridger shrugged slightly. "While your son is respected, that doesn't mean he doesn't have his share of enemies, if you catch my meaning."

"Jim Bridger is telling you the truth, Reverend," said Fitzpatrick. "While your son is an honorable man, some are not too fond of him or his friend Liam O'Reilly, mostly because they fear them."

"We understand," said the reverend. "And shall follow your advice."

Reverend and Mrs. Hancock thanked Bridger and Fitzpatrick for the advice and information and headed in the direction Bridger said the Cheyenne and Arapaho villages were camped. As they traveled, Reverend Hancock wondered how he was going to communicate with anyone from the two tribes, since no one in the family spoke their language. He mentioned as much to his wife and daughter, but everyone was so excited at the possibility of seeing Azariah again, they didn't seem to worry about the minor problem of communication or lack thereof.

"I'm sure there is someone among these people who speaks English and can tell us where Azariah is," said Jason.

At the mention of Azariah's name, a young Indian woman and her husband turned around as they passed by the reverend and his family. Young Caleb noticed their attention on them and informed the rest of the family as the Indian couple, who had a baby about the age of one going on two with them, approached. It was the woman who spoke. "We overheard you mention Azariah," she said in flawless English. "Would that be Azariah Hancock?"

"Why, yes," answered Reverend Hancock, who was impressed with the young Indian lady's English. "Are you friends of his?"

"More like family," said the Indian woman. "I am Blue-bird." She then introduced her husband, White Hawk, and their son Spotted Bear. While White Hawk spoke very little English, he understood what his wife was saying, and despite looking at Reverend Hancock and his family with a little suspicion, he couldn't help but notice a resemblance to Azariah.

"How do you know Azariah?" asked Bluebird.

It was Mother Abigail who answered. "He is our son."

Bluebird and White Hawk both looked surprised but quickly regained their composure. "You're Nehemiah and Abigail Hancock?" asked Bluebird. The good reverend and his wife nodded. Bluebird then turned to Little Abigail. "You must be his twin sister, Abigail."

Little Abigail gave a slight smile and nodded. "You said my brother is like family to you."

Bluebird nodded and said, "He and my mother's husband, Liam, are best friends."

"You mean Liam O'Reilly?" asked Reverend Hancock.

Bluebird nodded. "Come with us. Liam will take you to your son."

The Hancock family couldn't contain their excitement as they followed Bluebird and White Hawk to the Cheyenne encampment. When they arrived, Liam and Choke Cherry Woman had just finished eating breakfast and were about to head over to the Arapaho encampment to get Azariah and Sweet Grass to go to the trading tents.

With a smile on his face, the Irishman greeted his eldest stepdaughter and son-in-law. "Well, now, just who have you brought with you, Bluebird?"

"Father, this is Azariah's family."

Liam, Choke Cherry Woman, Little Fawn, and even Luke Medicine Horse looked surprised. Reverend Hancock quickly introduced himself as he extended his hand to the Irishman. Liam almost couldn't believe that he was standing before his best friend's father, who was taller than him by four inches. "My son's letter told us everything about you," said Reverend Hancock. "Will you kindly take us to him?"

"You haven't seen him yet?" asked Liam.

"No. Your daughter brought us to you and said that you would take us to him and his family," said Reverend Hancock.

"Then why are we standing here?" shouted an excited Choke Cherry Woman. "Let us reunite you with your son and meet your daughter-in-law and grandchildren!"

3

FAMILY REUNION

There was not a dull moment in the Arapaho encampment of Chief Red Hoof. The warrior was chosen by the people to be the new leader of the village not long before his grandfather, Chief White Antelope, passed on to the Happy Hunting Grounds three years previously. He and Azariah were the same age, and the latter was among Chief Red Hoof's staunchest supporters.

Azariah came to pay his respects to the young chief when he and his family arrived in the encampment for the Rendezvous a week prior, and he, along with two of his closest friends, Beaver and Otter Tail, would hunt with the chief to bring in much-needed meat while waiting for the fur trading caravan to arrive.

Azariah and his family were having breakfast with Chief Red Hoof when there was a commotion outside the chief's tipi. There was a knock on the flap, and the chief told whoever it was knocking to enter.

"Sorry for the intrusion," said Beaver, "but Raging Bull is here, and he has a surprise for He Who Walks Tall and his family." Everyone looked at Azariah, who looked confused, mainly because he never knew Liam to be one for surprises. "He wants you and every member of your family to come," said Beaver.

"This must be some surprise," said Chief Red Hoof.

"It better be," retorted Azariah. "I was about to enjoy this buffalo steak that your wife slaved over cooking." At that, everyone laughed as they exited the tipi. Since the surprise was for Azariah, he was the last one to leave.

Those present other than Sweet Grass and the children were Chief Red Hoof's wife, Morning Star, and Sweet Grass' parents, Two Hawks and Clay Basket, along with her brother, Howling Wolf and his wife, Prairie Bird Woman and their eleven-year-old son, Little Badger. They were the first to exit the tipi and notice the small group of whites standing next to Liam and Choke Cherry Woman.

Bluebird was whispering to the older white gentleman and the two white women standing with him while pointing at Sweet Grass and the children. Sweet Grass was staring closely at the white women and saw something familiar about them when Azariah exited the tipi from behind her and suddenly froze. She turned in time to see the shocked look on her husband's face as if he recognized the visitors.

Azariah thought he was staring at ghosts the minute he exited Chief Red Hoof's tipi and saw his parents for the first time in sixteen years. "You and the children wait here," he said to Sweet Grass in Arapaho. He slowly approached his parents, who by this time had tears in their eyes as they looked up at the approaching giant of a man—their long-lost son. Liam and Choke Cherry Woman helped clear a path for Azariah as he approached them. By this time, word of the newcomers had spread throughout the village, and everyone watched in anticipation as He Who Walks Tall approached his family. As he got closer to his parents, Azariah suddenly fell to his knees, with tears in his eyes.

"Father," he said aloud, only enough for his parents to hear. "Mother!"

Reverend and Mother Hancock both suddenly grabbed their son, wrapping their arms around his giant frame. "My son!" shouted Reverend Hancock. "My son!" The reverend pulled his son to stand at his full height, towering over his parents. "I thought we would never see your face again," said Reverend Hancock as he gently placed his palms on his son's face.

Azariah immediately hugged both parents as the villagers cheered and whooped in joy at the family reunion they were witnessing.

After what felt like an eternity, Azariah finally released his parents from his embrace, long enough to notice his twin sister. "Abigail!" he shouted as he picked her up in a bear hug.

With tears of joy streaming down her cheeks, Abigail just shouted her brother's name as the two siblings embraced for the first time in more than a decade. It was a joyous reunion for the Hancock family. When Azariah put Abigail down, he turned his attention to Jason Allen. No questions needed to be asked.

"It is good to see you again, Azariah," said Jason as he held out his hand.

"Likewise, brother," responded Azariah, who grabbed his brother-in-law and pulled him into a bear hug also, eliciting more cheers and whoops from the villagers.

When he put Jason down, Azariah quickly noticed his three nephews as Abigail introduced them to their uncle. Caleb, Abraham, and Jacob were all intimidated at first by the giant who was their mother's long-lost twin brother, but as Azariah held out his hand, six-year-old Jacob was the first to overcome his fear and accept his uncle's handshake. Caleb was next to introduce himself, followed by Abraham.

"It is a pleasure to meet all three of you fine young men," said Azariah. However, he quickly noticed a difference between the three boys. While Abraham and Jacob looked exactly like Jason, Caleb looked more like Abigail, but nothing like Jason at all. This did not go unnoticed by his sister or Jason. "How old are you, Caleb?"

A shiver of fear came down Little Abigail's spine as she saw the look of suspicion on her brother's face. "I will be sixteen in December, sir," answered Caleb. With that answer,

Azariah knew that Caleb was not Jason's son. "My father," said Caleb, "my real father was Belshazzar Jones."

Azariah turned to his sister and parents. The look of concern on their faces said it all, but then suddenly, Azariah smiled and turned back to his eldest nephew. "No, he wasn't," he said. Azariah suddenly pointed to Jason Allen and said, "That man is your real father, and you are my nephew. Nothing will ever change that." He then gave Caleb a bear hug and kissed him on his forehead after he released him. Azariah turned towards Jason and thanked him for what he did for Abigail and Caleb.

"I wish I could have done more," responded Jason.

Azariah smiled and said, "You have done enough. We're family now." After wiping the tears from his sister and mother's faces, it was Azariah's turn to introduce someone. "Mother, Father," he said. "There are some people very dear to me I want you to meet." He quickly turned around and ran towards Sweet Grass and the children. Taking his wife by the hand, he gently escorted her to meet his parents and sister. Both the good reverend and Mother Abigail were smiling from ear to ear as their son introduced his bride.

"Azariah, she is an angel from Heaven!" shouted Mother Abigail.

"I greet my husband's parents with great joy," said Sweet Grass.

Reverend Hancock gently placed both his hands on her shoulders and smiled before saying, "The joy is all ours, my daughter!" He then kissed her on her forehead before hugging her. He was about to introduce her to Little Abigail, Jason, and the boys when he felt not one but two tugs on his trousers. He looked down to find the twins, Abigail Little Flower and Solomon White Wolf, holding out their arms to him, much to the surprise of their parents. "I see these to be my grandchildren," said Reverend Hancock. "God's light shines in their eyes." He scooped up the twins in his arms and gave each of them a peck on the cheek.

"Are you our grandpa?" asked Little Flower.

"Yes, my little angel," answered Reverend Hancock. "I am your grandpa." With that, both Little Flower and her twin brother White Wolf gave the big white man a hug.

"You have two older grandchildren as well," said Sweet Grass. Azariah pointed to Adam Bear Claw and Sara Sunshine, who were standing next to grandfather Two Hawks and grandmother Clay Basket. They hesitated to approach these old white people who were their father's parents.

It was Mother Abigail who broke the ice and called to them. "Come, my angels, do not be afraid," she said. "Come, so that your grandfather and I can bless you."

With a little encouragement from not only their parents but from Two Hawks and Clay Basket, Bear Claw and Sunshine slowly approached their white grandmother for the first time. With tears in her eyes, Mother Abigail embraced them to her bosom and kissed both of them on their heads as she looked towards the heavens as if thanking the Creator for this day.

Adam Bear Claw, who, along with his siblings, had not had good experiences with their father's people, were both surprised and relieved at how this white woman who was his grandmother accepted him with such a loving embrace. At least that is what he felt from her as she held him and his sister. He could feel her love as tears continued to pour down her cheeks. Sara Sunshine was amazed as well, for she often wondered why her father never took them back East to the land he was born to visit his blood kin. Both children felt that maybe he believed that they, along with their mother, would not be accepted by their white relatives, but they were glad this was not the case.

Mother Abigail released her grip on the children and gently placed her hands on each of their faces. "Don't cry, Grandmother," said Adam as he wiped away the flowing tears from his grandmother's face.

Mother Abigail almost chuckled and smiled as she nodded. "I am just so happy to see you both," she said. "You look so much like your father."

"Mother, please don't insult them," joked Azariah. "They take after their mother as far as good looks are concerned."

Azariah received an elbow in his ribs from Sweet Grass, while his parents introduced their grandchildren to their Aunt Abigail, Uncle Jason, and their three cousins. Jacob, the boldest of the three boys, immediately ran up and hugged

Little Flower and White Wolf. Caleb and Adam sized each other up before exchanging handshakes, while Abraham, who was still overcoming his nervousness, stood behind his father, who was trying to get him to at least say hello.

"Now that we have you back in our arms again," said Reverend Hancock, "and laid eyes upon your wife and children, I can now die in peace."

Mother Abigail quickly gave her husband a swift kick in the shins for that comment. "How can you think of death at a joyous time like this?"

With that, everyone laughed at Mother Abigail's scolding, and Azariah just shook his head and said, "I'm glad some things never change."

Afterward, Azariah thanked Liam and Choke Cherry Woman for bringing his family safely to the village. Liam informed him that it was Bluebird and White Hawk who found them, which explained why some members from the Cheyenne encampment were there. As Azariah was introducing his family to everyone in the village, word had gotten to the Cheyenne village and beyond to the Rendezvous that the parents of He Who Walks Tall had come from the East. It had raised a lot of excitement. Even tribes who were traditional enemies of the Arapaho, Cheyenne, and their allies, the Lakota, were curious. While the Crow, Shoshone, Flathead, Ute, and Nez Perce had considered both Azariah and Liam as enemies just by their association with the Arapaho, Cheyenne, and Lakota alone, that didn't mean they didn't respect the two trappers, especially Azariah. His reputation as an honorable man was well known, and hearing that his blood kin had come to see him piqued their curiosity.

After introductions were made between the Hancocks and Sweet Grass' family, Azariah led his parents to Chief Red Hoof and the council. Reverend Hancock was impressed by the young chief and the many elders who sat on the village council.

"Welcome to our village, Father of He Who Walks Tall," said Chief Red Hoof in the Arapaho tongue.

Azariah translated the greeting to his father, who bowed and thanked the chief for the welcome. Then, Reverend Hancock asked Azariah to translate every word he was about to say to the chief. "Tell me, Great Chief, does my son serve your people well?"

Azariah translated his father's question, which astonished not only Red Hoof and the council but everyone who was in earshot. "Your son has brought great honor to my people," answered Chief Red Hoof. "He has hunted buffalo with us and at great risks to his own life, he has helped fight off our enemies and anyone who has a bad heart towards us."

Reverend Hancock smiled after his son finished translating what the chief had said. "I am happy that my son has been such a blessing for you and your people, and I thank you and Raging Bull, along with the Cheyenne, for taking him in as one of your own. It pained his mother and me when he had to leave us due to forces beyond our control, but I am grateful and humbled that God has given him a place, a people, and a family that he can call his own."

After Azariah had translated his father's last statement, Reverend Hancock raised his hands to the sky and spoke: "May the God of Abraham, Isaac, and Jacob rain down showers of blessings upon you and your people. May your people live forever, and may He protect your people and your allies from all harm, and may He strike down those who wish to commit evil against you. For this I pray in His name, Amen."

After the blessing was translated into Arapaho by Azariah and into Cheyenne by Liam to the benefit of some of the Cheyenne visitors, everyone stood there in astonishment. Many of the elders, including the medicine man, Wandering Bear, a long-time friend of Azariah, were extremely impressed as well as amazed. When Chief Red Hoof realized that this strange white man whom he had just met had blessed him, his people, and their allies, he did the only thing he could think of. He said, "Thank you."

4

TWO WORLDS, ONE FAMILY

Later that evening, a great feast was held in honor of Azariah's family. Visitors came from not just the Cheyenne and Lakota, but even many trappers and individuals from other tribes at the Rendezvous who were only acquaintances came to visit.

Azariah's father was becoming a massive center of attention as he was telling stories about his son when he was a child back in Maryland. Always eager to help embarrass his young pupil and best friend, Liam O'Reilly translated what the good reverend was saying into both Cheyenne and Arapaho, while using sign language so everyone could get a huge laugh as Reverend Hancock told some embarrassing stories about his son.

"So there is Azariah," said Reverend Hancock, "naked as

a newborn babe in front of his poor mama and all her fine church lady friends!"

Everyone except Azariah got a good laugh. "I was three years old, Pa," moaned Azariah.

The reverend looked at him in mock anger. "Azariah, how many times have I told you that lying lips are an abomination unto the Lord!" With a huge grin, the reverend turned back to the crowd and said, "He was eight!"

Azariah acted like he was going to throw a moccasin at his father as he and everyone laughed. "You are going to pay for that!"

Reverend Hancock then turned to Sweet Grass. "Now, Sweet Grass, tell me the truth. Does my son serve you well?"

"Nehemiah!" shouted Mother Abigail.

"Now, now, Abigail," said Reverend Hancock. "I have gone through a lot of trouble trying to set a good example for our only son on how a man is to be a good husband. You wouldn't want all that time and effort to go to waste now, would you?"

Sweet Grass giggled as her mother-in-law threw up her hands in the air as a sign of embarrassment at the man they both loved dearly. "Your son has made me the happiest woman ever."

Azariah smiled and blushed at his wife's answer.

"But can he cook?" asked Reverend Hancock. "A good husband must always know how to cook for his woman."

"That's enough out of you, Nehemiah Job Hancock!"

shouted Mother Abigail as she grabbed her husband by his ear and dragged him back to their seat of honor next to Chief Red Hoof and his family.After everyone got a good laugh between eating and drinking, conversations were going on between some of the families, the council members, and even the Hancock and O'Reilly families about where to go after the Rendezvous was over and where the village would be making the winter encampment. Azariah was quiet but happily content now that his entire family was together. He and Sweet Grass had already informed her parents that they might tag along with the village for a while after the Rendezvous, before returning to their cabin in the Beartooth Mountains.

Chief Red Hoof and the council decided that, as blood relatives of He Who Walks Tall, the Hancocks were automatically adopted members of the Arapaho Nation and were more than welcome to stay with the village for as long as they wished. Azariah translated this to his family, and they were more than grateful. Both Mother and Little Abigail were getting to know Sweet Grass, Clay Basket, Prairie Bird Woman, Choke Cherry Woman, Bluebird, and Little Fawn, helping with the cooking and passing out dinner according to both Arapaho and Cheyenne customs.

After dinner, Azariah, Liam, Reverend Hancock, along with Jason and the boys, sat around the fire with Two Hawks, Howling Wolf, Chief Red Hoof, Beaver, Otter Tail, and the medicine man, Wandering Bear. Reverend Hancock and

LEROY A. PETERS

Wandering Bear quickly struck up a discussion on religion, both from the Arapaho and the white man's points of view. The good reverend was very curious about what Indians, in general, believed as far as religion was concerned because all he had ever heard was mostly propaganda.

"So you are a holy man?" asked Wandering Bear.

Reverend Hancock was getting used to the medicine man speaking English, forgetting that his son had lived among the Arapaho for sixteen years. "I wouldn't go that far," he said. "But, yes, I do consider myself a man of God."

Wandering Bear thought for a moment. Just as Reverend Hancock has thought about Indians and their way of life, the Arapaho medicine man was curious about the white man's religion that they called Christianity. All he knew about it was from what Azariah and Liam had told him.

"In your religion," asked Reverend Hancock, "what name do you call God?"

"We call him the Man Above. Your son believes that He and the god you call Jesus Christ are the same god."

Reverend Hancock looked at Azariah for a moment, who just shrugged. "Considering that we believe that Jesus Christ is way above the clouds and that you call him the Man Above, that is something I cannot argue against." Unlike most whites, especially those claiming to be Christians, Nehemiah Hancock did not have a bigoted and ignorant view of non-white people, especially blacks and Indians. At most, he was curious about other religions. While he believed that Chris-

40

tianity was the right one, and that the Bible was God's word, he did not nor would not put down or judge other people's religions.

Azariah watched and listened closely as his father and the medicine man talked. He remembered when he first came out West, still a greenhorn trapper, learning how Indians viewed God. He quickly accepted that their religion and Christianity were probably the same or extremely similar, at least from what he saw living among both the Arapaho and Cheyenne.

"Is it true that your people take scalps from an enemy?" asked the reverend.

His father's question quickly interrupted Azariah's train of thought as both Chief Red Hoof and Wandering Bear nodded their answer.

"Why?"

Azariah at first started to get nervous but quickly realized that his father was not passing judgment but asking out of curiosity. Jason listened intently while Caleb, Abraham and Jacob gave their full and undivided attention to the question.

"It is the way of things," said Two Hawks. "To take the scalp of an enemy is considered an honor."

"Counting coup, we call it," added Howling Wolf. "We take their scalp among other things from their body, so that their spirits may forever wander in this world and never see the Happy Hunting Grounds."

"Sounds pretty barbaric," said Jason.

"White men do it, too," said Liam.

By this time, the women had arrived around the campfire and were listening to the conversation.

"Still doesn't make it right," said Reverend Hancock, "no matter who does it."

"Isn't mutilating the body of an enemy in the Bible, Grandpa?" asked Caleb.

"If it is, I don't believe it was men of God committing it."

"Oh, yes, it was," interjected Sweet Grass. "The bride price for your King David to Saul's daughter was one hundred foreskins of the enemy."

Both Reverend Hancock and Mother Abigail looked at their daughter-in-law, clearly impressed with her statement. "You know your Bible," said Mother Abigail.

"I have had a good teacher," said Sweet Grass as she sat down next to her husband. Azariah placed his huge arm around her and gave her a peck on the cheek.

Reverend Hancock just smiled and shook his head and said, "We are not all that different, after all, and you are right, Sweet Grass. If memory serves, David got two hundred enemy foreskins instead of the required one hundred."

"Uncle Azariah," said young Jacob, "have you and Mr. O'Reilly taken scalps?"

"Have you been on raids?" added Abraham.

"Boys!" scolded their mother, but Azariah gently raised his hand before answering.

"The answer to both questions is yes."

Mother Abigail tried in vain to hide her surprise at her son's revelation. However, neither Azariah's father nor Jason were surprised. "As Two Hawks said, it is the way of things, and when you take the life of an enemy who is trying to kill you, just killing him isn't enough."

"Surely you don't believe that mutilating them would prevent them from entering the afterlife?" asked Jason.

Azariah just shrugged. "It doesn't matter if I believe in it or not, but the Arapaho, Cheyenne, and most of the tribes believe in it," he said. "It is a different world out here, and I am not about to try and judge it by our standards or change it, for that matter."

"Son," said Mother Abigail, "do you take any joy in killing other men?" Everyone could see the look of concern on his mother's face, even the good reverend. While he understood what kind of man his son had grown into, he shared his wife's concern.

"There have been some men who I have enjoyed not just killing but torturing before they died," said Azariah. "Either way, they were evil men, and the world is a better place without them."

"How many men have you killed, Uncle Azariah?" asked Abraham enthusiastically.

"Okay, that's enough questions," interrupted Jason. "Time for bed."

"But Pa," whined Jacob. "Things were just getting good."

"Do as your father says," admonished Little Abigail. "Off to bed."

Abraham and Jacob knew better than to test both of their parents. Since the family was staying in the lodge of Sweet Grass' parents, Clay Basket offered to take the boys back and tuck them in. Azariah thought it was getting late as well and instructed Sara, Abigail, and Solomon to go with their grandmother and cousins. The three children did, but not before giving Grandma and Grandpa Hancock a kiss goodnight.

Reverend Hancock beamed with pride as he watched his grandchildren walk with Clay Basket into the night to where they would be sleeping. Caleb and Adam convinced their parents to stay a little longer. The two cousins were getting to know each other very well and had asked Howling Wolf if they could go hunting with him and some of the warriors in the morning, with their father's permission, of course.

"It's okay with me," said Azariah.

"I think I will join you," added Jason. "I have never hunted buffalo."

"It's dangerous," said Liam. "But it is worth it."

"I think I'll go as well," said Reverend Hancock. "That is, if it is okay with you, Howling Wolf?"

"You would be welcome. The more men, the better."

"Nehemiah Job Hancock," nagged Mother Abigail. "You are too old to be involved in hunting, especially something as dangerous as a buffalo!"

The reverend just rolled his eyes and sighed. "You see what I have to go through?" Everyone laughed.

"A man such as yourself should count himself blessed to have a wife who cares," said Two Hawks.

"I can't argue with that," responded Reverend Hancock. "Abigail, how do you know that hunting buffalo is dangerous anyway?"

"Mr. O'Reilly just said it was," answered Mother Abigail. "Besides, any beast that is three times the size of a horse is no gentle giant."

"Your son is three times the size of a horse," said Sweet Grass. "And he is a gentle giant."

Azariah turned beet red, while Liam, Choke Cherry Woman and everyone except Mother and Little Abigail guffawed. "Lord have mercy," said Mother Abigail.

"Amen and hallelujah!" shouted Sweet Grass, who winked at her husband.

5

THE HUNT

The very next morning, Howling Wolf, Beaver, and Otter Tail were up and ready to get the hunting party together, when Azariah, his father, Jason, Adam, and Caleb joined them for the morning hunt.

"Ready whenever you are, gentlemen," said Jason.

"More men are coming," said Beaver. "Hunting buffalo is very dangerous even with the number that we have."

"I can imagine," responded Reverend Hancock.

It was at that moment, Liam and young Luke showed up with friends from the Cheyenne village. Azariah immediately recognized He Dog, Liam's father-in-law from his first marriage, along with his sons, Thunder Cloud, Pawnee Killer, and Spotted Eagle, along with Spotted Eagle's son, Sparrow. Choke Cherry Woman's father, Yellow Hawk, and her brother, Red Moon, were also present and had been long-time friends and allies of Azariah. Among the Cheyenne, Sparrow was Azariah's closest friend since they were teenagers. Azariah had saved Sparrow from a buffalo when they first met each other sixteen years ago. Sparrow mentioned as much to Azariah's father and brother-in-law when they arrived for the hunt.

"It appears you have done a lot over the years when it comes to making friends," chuckled Reverend Hancock.

"Do unto others as you would have them do unto you," quoted Azariah.

Reverend Hancock sighed. "The world would be a much better place to live in if we all practiced that."

"I agree," said He Dog.

Like many of the men who had just met Azariah's kin, he was eager to get to know them and was excited to be hunting buffalo with them. He had heard that the reverend was a holy man or a white medicine man. Despite the latter denying being either, He Dog wanted to know more. He was impressed when Liam told him about how the reverend blessed both the Arapaho and Cheyenne Nations, as well as their allies, the Lakota, and condemned those who wished ill will against them. Never had he heard a white man doing that for them—the opposite, in fact.

Liam quickly introduced the rest of the Cheyenne hunting party to the reverend, Jason and Caleb, before plans on how the hunt would go was laid out. He Dog and Yellow Hawk led the hunting party out of the village and onto the plains to find the buffalo herd. It wasn't long before they found what they were looking for—a vast herd of at least a hundred or more buffalo bulls, cows, and calves about six miles west from the villages and the Rendezvous site.

While Reverend Hancock, Jason, and Caleb had seen buffalo on their way West, they couldn't help but continue to be in awe of the great beasts. "Magnificent," said the reverend.

"And delicious," added Liam.

"How are we going to hunt them?" asked Caleb.

"Just follow our lead, nephew," said Azariah.

With that, Howling Wolf gave a war cry, and the whole hunting party charged into the herd, causing it to stampede. Watching how Liam, Azariah, and the Arapaho and Cheyenne warriors fired their rifles, bows, and arrows at their intended targets, Reverend Hancock, Jason, and Caleb followed their examples, each choosing a target. Reverend Hancock managed to fire his Kentucky rifle into a cow, the musket ball finding its mark, hitting a vital organ.

Thunder Cloud and Pawnee Killer witnessed him accomplish this and shouted their approval, congratulating him. Jason and Caleb were having a more difficult time. Both fired their rifles into a bull, but the beast seemed to be impervious to the shots as he continued to run away with the rest of the herd. They were also having a hard time reloading while riding on the back of a fast-moving horse. Azariah and Adam both grinned and shook their heads at their kin's predicament but were impressed that they didn't stop trying to kill the retreating beast.

"Why don't you show them how it is done?" said Azariah to his son.

Adam Bear Claw smiled and nodded before he rode towards his uncle and cousin and offered to help them catch their intended target. The trio had caught up to the wounded bull, who by this time had slowed down but was still running away from them. Adam had instructed them to shoot for the lungs, into the ribs. Heeding that instruction, Jason and Caleb fired two more shots from their rifles into the bull. This time, the beast went down.

The hunt was a success. When all was said and done, there were ten buffaloes down—six cows and four bulls. Thunder Cloud and Pawnee Killer were telling everyone how the good Reverend Hancock brought down his first buffalo with one shot from horseback. Reverend Hancock was a little embarrassed by the praise, but Azariah and Liam told him that it was nothing to be embarrassed about. Even Jason and Caleb patted him on the back and said that he did way better than what they accomplished on the hunt.

He Dog walked up to the cow that the reverend had shot and cut out her heart. He offered the still-steaming organ to Reverend Hancock, who had a confused look on his face.

"He is offering you to take a bite out of it first," said Azariah.

"Me?"

"It's your cow, Pa," said Azariah. "You get first dibs."

"But it's not even cooked."

"When it comes to buffalo liver, tongue and heart, you eat them raw," said Liam. "Trust me, Reverend, you best take a bite."

Sensing that to refuse would be an insult, Reverend Hancock accepted the buffalo heart from He Dog and took a small bite as Jason and Caleb watched, somewhat disgusted.

"How does it taste, Grandpa?" asked Caleb.

"Salty... but good!"

Reverend Hancock took another bite, this time a bigger one, and smiled as he chewed, blood dripping from his mouth down into his beard. The warriors whooped while Liam and Azariah smiled. Reverend Hancock offered the buffalo heart to Jason and Caleb, but the former shook his head; however, Caleb accepted the heart from his grandfather and took a bite.

"It tastes better than chicken," he said before giving it to Adam.

With the hunting done, the butchering needed to begin. Adam, Caleb, and Sparrow volunteered to ride back to the villages to retrieve help for the butchering. The hunters were just starting to skin the fourth buffalo when the combined Arapaho and Cheyenne villages arrived. The women immediately got started on the butchering. Not wanting to be idle, Mother and Little Abigail followed Sweet Grass and Choke Cherry Woman's example on how to butcher a buffalo. Within minutes, they were working side by side with the Arapaho and Cheyenne women, blood covering their arms, faces, and dresses by the time they were finished. Jacob and Abraham watched their mother and grandmother covered in blood; when everyone was done, the boys looked shocked and were scared even to approach them, but their father put them at ease as he told them about the hunt and how their Grandpa Hancock brought down a cow with one shot.

Azariah and Liam had taken the hearts, livers, and tongues from the buffaloes they had killed and offered a heart each to their wives and children to eat. At first, Mother and Little Abigail were horrified as they watched Sweet Grass, Choke Cherry Woman and the children eat some of the raw organs, but it was Reverend Hancock who encouraged his wife and daughter to try it. "When in Rome, do what the Romans do," he said and offered his wife a buffalo liver from the cow he killed.

"You can't be serious?" said Mother Abigail as she looked at the liver.

"Try it, Abigail," said Reverend Hancock. He took a bite from the liver before offering it to his wife again, and she relented. After taking a small bite, she offered it to their daughter.

"How does it taste?" asked Little Abigail.

"Not bad."

At that, Little Abigail took a bite and her expression indicated that it wasn't awful.

By the end of the day, there was enough meat to hold a feast for both the Cheyenne and Arapaho villages. Thunder Cloud and Pawnee Killer spread the word around the Cheyenne how the father of He Who Walks Tall killed his first buffalo with one shot from horseback while riding. Liam had informed the good reverend that he would be expected to tell the story of his feat and embellish it.

Reverend Hancock realized that Thunder Cloud and Pawnee Killer had done him a favor and had raised his status among the two tribes. He was both flattered and concerned, since he never considered himself a braggart, but both Azariah and Liam assured him that it wasn't bragging if it was true.

Before the feast started, Clay Basket and Prairie Bird Woman had made two new dresses for Mother and Little Abigail to help replace their dresses that got messed up during the butchering of the buffalo. When mother and daughter presented themselves before their husbands dressed in their new Arapaho dresses with their hair braided in two, Reverend Hancock and Jason just gawked.

"Well," asked Mother Abigail. "How do we look?"

"Like angels," said Jason, recovering from his gawking.

"I agree," said Reverend Hancock. He then walked up to

his wife and whispered, "Is that dress easier to take off than your other ones?"

Mother Abigail punched him playfully in the stomach as he laughed before he wrapped his arms around her and kissed her. Jason did the same with Little Abigail, before they all decided to join the rest of the family for the big feast.

6

THE DREAM

After Rendezvous broke up, the fur trading companies headed back east to St. Louis with their fortunes, while the trappers with their new supplies for the next year headed west to find new trapping grounds. The many tribes present also left the Rendezvous site to go to their winter encampments and prepare for the upcoming winter.

Among the Arapaho village of Red Hoof, Azariah Hancock and his family decided to travel with the village to the winter encampment before returning to their cabin in the Beartooth Mountains. Liam O'Reilly and his family stopped by to say their goodbyes before going with their Cheyenne relatives to their winter encampment.

"You're not coming with us?" asked Mother Abigail.

"We will see each other again soon," answered Liam.

"We too live in the Beartooth Mountains, not far from Azariah and Sweet Grass."

"Oh," said Mother Abigail.

"Uncle Azariah said that the mountains are unlike any we have seen back east," said Caleb.

"He's right," said Liam. "It is an absolute Garden of Eden."

"Well, I'm looking forward to the trapping lessons from both you and Azariah, Mr. O'Reilly," said Jason. "I mean, if we are all going to be living together with y'all, we might as well learn how to survive out here."

Young Abraham was horrified. "You mean we're not going back home to Maryland?"

"This is our home now, Abraham," said Little Abigail. "This is our family now."

"What about Auntie Sweet Grass' people?" asked Jacob. "Aren't we staying with them?"

"For the time being," answered Azariah. "After we help set their winter encampment, then we'll go to our home in the Beartooth Mountains."

"Will Uncle Two Hawks and Aunt Clay Basket come with us?" asked Jacob.

"Would you like my parents to come?" asked Sweet Grass.

Jacob grinned from ear to ear and nodded. Unlike his brother, Abraham, he had become close to not just his cousins and Sweet Grass' family, but he had gotten used to being around the Arapaho and Cheyenne children and adults, which amazed his parents and grandparents.

Abraham was having none of it. He missed Maryland and didn't like it out West, and he let everyone know it. "I don't want to live out here. I want to go home to Grandpa and Grandma Allen!"

"Abraham!" shouted Jason. "That's enough out of you!"

"Easy, Jason," said Reverend Hancock. "He is only seven. He is too young to understand."

"We told him and his brothers that if we found Azariah, we weren't coming back to Maryland."

"I know," said the reverend. "But it is still not an easy thing to put on a child that young."

"Father is right," said Azariah. "While I appreciate all of you coming and living with us, change is not an easy thing for a child."

While everyone was trying to calm down Abraham, Caleb walked over to Little Fawn. "I was hoping to get to spend some time with you," he said. "Maybe you can teach me the Cheyenne language."

Little Fawn smiled. "I would like that."

The young man quickly bowed his head and turned red. Since they had first met, Caleb noticed how beautiful Little Fawn was, but the only time he managed to chat with her was when their families were around each other. "I figured I am going to be learning to speak Arapaho. I might as well learn to speak Cheyenne."

"I can teach you both," said Little Fawn.

"Really?" shouted an excited Caleb.

Little Fawn was giggling when everyone turned their attention towards the two teenagers.

"What has gotten you so excited, nephew?" asked Azariah.

"Oh, nothing."

"I offered to teach him the Cheyenne and Arapaho tongues," Little Fawn explained.

"Oh, you did, did you?" said Liam. He was a little concerned. Though he had nothing personal against Caleb, he being Azariah's nephew and all, he had always been protective of Bluebird and Little Fawn ever since he married their mother.

"Mr. O'Reilly, is it okay with you that I come to court your daughter?" asked Caleb.

No one was more shocked by the request that Caleb had made more than his mother and Liam. Jason was beaming with pride. While Caleb was not his son by blood, he loved him all the same, and for a while he was starting to worry about the youth because he had never shown much interest in women until now. Sister Abigail was concerned for a different reason. While she had no racial bigotry against blacks and Indians and loved Sweet Grass and her people, she wasn't sure how she really felt about her son mixing with an Indian, even if she was the daughter of her brother's best friend. However, she kept those feelings to herself.

"If your parents are okay with it, then I have no objections to you courting my daughter," said Liam. "What say you, Mr. and Mrs. Allen?"

"I will defy no man concerning his daughter," said Jason. "But if you have no objections to our son courting your daughter, then neither do we."

"I noticed you have been quiet," said Liam to Azariah.

"Hey, she ain't my daughter!"

Everyone laughed at Azariah's comment.

About a week after the village left the Green River, they arrived at the headwaters of the Arkansas. It was there that the village would make their winter encampment. After everything was set up, a council was held and it was decided the men would go at first light to find and hunt buffalo for meat in order to be ready for winter. Reverend Hancock above all was excited to go hunting again with the warriors and his son and grandsons. Mother and Sister Abigail were getting settled into life as adopted Arapaho women. Mother Abigail in particular was becoming a surrogate mother, along with Clay Basket, to many of the village children, some of whom were orphans. Reverend Hancock, Jason, Caleb, Abraham and Jacob had gotten new buckskin clothes made for them before they left Rendezvous and also got new weapons such as Hawken rifles and pistols as well Arkansas toothpicks. Azariah and Adam showed them, especially the boys, how to use them and reload them. Reverend Hancock and Jason both hoped that they would never have to use them on another person, but they were realistic.

The only person in the family who was not happy about their new life in the West was seven-year-old Abraham Allen. He missed Maryland, his grandparents, cousins and the rich life that his father's family provided. He never kept quiet about it, and ever since they left Rendezvous, he would frequently have temper tantrums about wanting to go home and even threatened to run away. On more than one occasion, his parents would give him a spanking, which shocked many of their Arapaho friends and relatives. Sweet Grass and her mother remembered being told by Azariah how whites disciplined their children, but they didn't believe him until they saw Jason put a switch to Abraham's backside one day for being rude.

Jason and Sister Abigail were just as surprised to realize that Indians, at least the Arapaho, didn't beat their children as a form of punishment. They were surprised because every child in the Arapaho village appeared to be well behaved, more so than their own kids. They asked Sweet Grass how she and Azariah disciplined their kids and they explained by either teasing, or taking things that they favored away from them, such as a favorite toy, for example.

"You never once spanked your children, Azariah?" asked a surprised Jason.

"I have been tempted, believe me," answered Azariah.

"But how the Arapaho discipline their children, you have to admit, it does work."

"Try it," said Sweet Grass.

Jason and Abigail decided to give it a try, but both Reverend Hancock, Mother Abigail and even Two Hawks and Clay Basket offered some parental advice, and they all agreed that they should talk to Abraham and listen to him. Even though he was a child, he was not a baby, and he was not dumb or deaf. He was at an age where he didn't understand why he couldn't have everything he wished for, but the best way to make him understand was by talking to him and listening, as well.

With the help of Sweet Grass' parents, Jason and Abigail managed to make Abraham understand why they were staying with Uncle Azariah and the Araphoes, and they listened to him about how much he missed his blood kin back east. Deep down, Jason had to admit that he missed his parents and brothers and sisters, but he accepted the fact that when he uprooted his family to move West and be reunited with his brother-in-law, he knew that he would not see his kin again. However, he hadn't taken into consideration how much that would affect his children, especially Abraham.

Grandmother Clay Basket and Grandfather Two Hawks were a huge help, for they chatted with Abraham after his parents talked to him and let him know how much he and his brothers were loved by them as if they were their own children. It took some time, but Abraham soon became accustomed to his new life, and before long he joined Jacob in frolicking and playing with the village children. He even took a fancy to horse racing. Since he loved horses, Azariah and Howling Wolf taught him and some of the boys who were coming of age how to ride horses bareback, and Abraham was becoming an adept student, something that did not go unnoticed.

Wandering Bear and Two Hawks gave Jason some sound advice. "Keep a close eye on that one," said Two Hawks. "He is young, but he is already riding like an Arapaho."

"He might grow into a great warrior, like his uncle," added Wandering Bear.

Jason took the two elders' advice to heart and thanked them.

For the next couple of weeks, the Arapaho encampment got settled for the winter, even though it was still August. Successful hunts were made and food was being stored for the winter. It was around that time, Azariah and Sweet Grass informed the family that it was time to leave and head back north to their cabin in the Beartooth Mountains. Liam and Choke Cherry Woman would meet them there. Two Hawks and Clay Basket asked if they could come, which to no one's surprise their daughter and son-in-law said yes, and young Jacob cheerfully screamed out WAUGH! Out of all the Allen boys, he was the one who had gotten close to the Arapaho sub-chief and his wife, whom he affectionately called Uncle Two Hawks and Aunt Clay Basket. Reverend Hancock and

Mother Abigail, along with Jason, Sister Abigail and the boys were just as excited to head north to their new permanent home. It was decided that they would stay in tipis until cabins were built for the Hancocks and the Allens, which suited everyone just fine. Jason and Caleb had been on enough successful hunts with Azariah and Adam accumulating enough animal skins to set up a tipi and live in it all winter.

Three days before they were to depart, Reverend Hancock had a dream. Somewhere farther southeast, there were two Indian villages. One was Arapaho and the other Cheyenne. It was a cold morning and the reverend stood at the opposite end of the villages and he could feel the cold as if it were real. Suddenly, he saw white men in blue uniforms approaching the villages, sneaking upon them. Some of the soldiers appeared to have been drunk, but either way they didn't appear to be friendly or in a good mood. Suddenly a heavyset man with a beard and receding hairline who appeared to be their leader shouted, "Charge!" and ordered his men to attack the peaceful, sleeping villages. He told his men to slaughter every man, woman and child. The man shouted, "Nits make lice!"

The horror that Reverend Hancock would witness before him was indescribable. Pregnant women had their bellies ripped open by sabers, children younger than Abigail and Solomon were gunned down and some had skulls crushed. Indian men trying to protect their families from this unprovoked attack were gunned down and scalped like dogs.

Reverend Hancock suddenly screamed, "NOOOO! MY GOD, NOOO!" He then woke up in a cold sweat, frightening Mother Abigail and the children.

"Nehemiah!" she said in a panic. "Are you all right?"

"No," he said. "It was terrible." Reverend Hancock suddenly stopped and rushed outside while still in his long johns.

Azariah, who heard his father's scream from the next lodge, rushed out to check on him.

"What is it?"

"A dream," said Reverend Hancock. "A terrible dream. I must speak with the elders."

"Whoa," said Azariah, putting his hands on his father's shoulder. "What for?"

"Trouble is coming to the red man."

7

PREDICTING THE FUTURE

Meanwhile, farther north near the Powder River in the Cheyenne village, the O'Reilly family were also helping their Cheyenne relatives and friends prepare for the winter before heading back to their cabin in the Beartooth Mountains.

Young Little Fawn, now in her fourteenth winter, couldn't stop thinking about Caleb Hancock. While their families were together at the Rendezvous, she remembered how polite and gentle he was when he approached her. Despite the fact that they were never alone together, it didn't stop the two teenagers from getting to know each other. This didn't go unnoticed by Choke Cherry Woman, who approved of the possible courtship between Azariah's nephew and her daughter.

Liam was another matter. He had always been protective of the girls when it came to the opposite sex. Choke Cherry

Woman remembered when White Hawk came to court Blue-bird, Liam had the look as if he wanted to scalp the young warrior. Yellow Hawk, who was Liam's father-in-law, would tease him, saying, "Now you know how I felt when you were chasing after her mother!" Either way, White Hawk turned out to be a good catch for Bluebird and an excellent father to their young son, Spotted Bear. Liam's problem was that he never got over the fact that his little girls were now young women. Bluebird had proudly given him a grandson and Little Fawn was now at the age to be courted. When he really thought about it, which young man was more suited to court his younger daughter than the nephew of his best friend and pupil? From what Liam had seen, Caleb was a decent young man from an excellent family, and for some reason Liam knew that if Caleb was going to court Little Fawn, then he would be able to protect her. He mentioned as much to Choke Cherry Woman.

Back at the Arapaho encampment, Reverend Hancock was standing before Chief Red Hoof and the council. With Azariah translating, he told the horrible dream and explained everything that happened.

"I believe what I have dreamt is the vision of the future," he said. "I pray that I am wrong."

After Azariah finished translating, it was Wandering Bear who spoke. "What if you're not wrong?"

"How can you be sure that he is not wrong, Wandering Bear?" asked Chief Red Hoof.

The Arapaho medicine man was quiet for a moment. Everyone in the village surrounding the council listened intently for his response. "I never told anyone this," said Wandering Bear. "But when I was a boy, I had the exact same vision that the father of He Who Walks Tall just had, and I never told anyone because I didn't want to believe it."

Reverend Hancock almost collapsed. He had grown to love the people of the village of Red Hoof, who accepted him and his family and treated them like their own family. He believed that this was his doing.

"We should never have come," he said. "I have brought a plague upon your people!"

"It is not your fault that the Man Above has given you a vision, White Medicine Eagle," said Wandering Bear. When both Reverend Hancock and his son looked at the medicine man with confusion, he just smiled. "That is your name now," he said. "For the Man Above has blessed you with a gift, and you are wise in telling us this vision, even if it is a bad one."

"I can't let this vision come to pass," said Reverend Hancock. "I *won't* let it come to pass."

"And what can you do, White Medicine Eagle?" asked Two Hawks. "What can any man do, when he has been given a vision that you have been given?"

"If my father's vision is a vision of what is to come, then we will fight," said Azariah.

"You are willing to kill another white man to protect our people?" asked Chief Red Hoof.

Azariah was almost hurt by the question. "I already have, in defense of my family and in defense of this village."

"There is more, I fear," said Reverend Hancock. "If what I dreamt is true, that means there'll be bloodshed from both sides, the red and white, and I have seen what that does to a man."

"So have I, Father," said Azariah.

"No... I am talking about killing women and children, the most vulnerable among us. I have seen it committed by both white men and by red men!" All was quiet for the moment before Reverend Hancock spoke again. "I believe that my vision was a warning," he said. "If war comes to not just the Arapahoes, but all the tribes, the most vulnerable on both sides will suffer. I vowed never to go through that again, nor do I want my children and grandchildren to go through that."

"If your vision is true, White Medicine Eagle," said Chief Red Hoof, "what do you suggest?"

"For starters," answered the reverend, "don't trust the white man. Make peace with them and try to keep the peace, but don't trust him to keep it."

When Azariah was done translating, everyone was surprised, except Two Hawks, Wandering Bear and Azariah.

"But you are white yourself, my friend," said Chief Red Hoof.

"All the more reason why I am warning you," responded the reverend. "No one has caused me and my family more pain and suffering than my own kind."

The elders and Chief Red Hoof murmured amongst themselves. Reverend Hancock, now called White Medicine Eagle, sat back down next to his son. To Azariah, he looked like he had aged ten years. Wandering Bear and Two Hawks both looked at him and nodded their approval. They knew that he cared greatly about the welfare of the people and he didn't want anything horrible to happen. But if his dream was a vision of what was to come, how could anyone change it or stop it? That was the question on everybody's mind.

8

GOING HOME

Two days later, Azariah and his family packed up and headed north towards the Beartooth Mountains. They said goodbye to their friends and relatives in the village of Red Hoof and were on the trail. Two Hawks and Clay Basket had made this journey many times before as they accompanied their daughter and her husband to their cabin. Their grandchildren always enjoyed it when their grandparents visited or vice versa, but now it was different because their father's family was with them and coming into the mountains for the first time.

Reverend Hancock, Mother Abigail, Jason, Sister Abigail and the boys all looked in awe and wonder at the Rocky Mountains as they followed Azariah, Sweet Grass and the children in a single file. The animals buzzed as birds sang and chipmunks were running to and fro, collecting acorns and other nuts for the upcoming winter. Jason and Caleb remembered what Azariah told them about listening to the sounds around you. If it was quiet, that meant danger was about. But if it was noisy like it was at the moment, that meant everything was safe.

"I miss Gideon," said Adam suddenly.

"Who is Gideon?" asked Mother Abigail.

"He was our dog. He passed on about three winters ago."

"He was old," said Azariah. "But he was a loyal friend."

Reverend Hancock and Mother Abigail could sense sadness in the voices of both their son and grandson. Azariah had fond memories of the dog that Sweet Grass had given him when they first met so many years ago. He was a puppy then, but as he got older he was a loyal pet and the family loved him.

"Uncle Azariah," shouted Caleb. "Over there!"

Not more than three hundred yards away near a berry bush was a grizzly and two cubs. Abraham and Jacob froze in fear as they sat on their saddles next to their mother, while Jason and Caleb had their Hawken rifles at the ready. Azariah signaled them to hold their fire. The mother grizzly was on her hind legs, sniffing the air. It was a tense situation and no one moved. Suddenly, one of the cubs attempted to approach the caravan, but its mother suddenly got back down on all fours and moved in front of it.

As she stood between her cubs and the humans,

Reverend Hancock whispered to Two Hawks, "What is she waiting for?"

"She is deciding if we are a threat or not," said Two Hawks. "Right now, we are too far away to be any threat but that does not mean she will not charge."

Grizzly bears had poor eyesight, but they made up for that with a strong sense of smell. Despite that, most adult females weighed between two hundred ninety to up to four hundred pounds and adult males weighed between four hundred and nearly eight hundred pounds. They could also run up to thirty-five miles per hour. For what felt like an hour, but was actually just over a minute, the she-grizzly evaluated the group but determined the humans were too far away to be any threat and were not approaching. However, she was not taking any chances and corralled her cubs away from them towards the forest.

Azariah breathed a sigh of relief. "That was close."

"What was that, Uncle Azariah?" asked Abraham.

"A grizzly bear," he said. "The most dangerous animal in these parts."

"She-grizzlies with cubs are the most dangerous," said Sweet Grass. "They have to be, because male grizzlies will kill the cubs."

"Interesting," said Reverend Hancock.

"I take it that could have ended badly," said Sister Abigail.

Azariah nodded. "She obviously believed that we were no

threat and too far away, but if she had wanted to, that wouldn't have stopped her from charging towards us." Azariah looked at the sky and figured it was still early, so signaled his family to continue up the pass.

Meanwhile, near the Powder River, the O'Reilly family were just leaving the Cheyenne village of Black Cloud. Liam and Choke Cherry Woman had said goodbye to the kin and friends before heading west to the Beartooth Mountains. Their cabin was three miles from the Hancocks' cabin and they were anxious to get home. Accompanying them was Bluebird and White Hawk and their son Spotted Bear. This would be the little tyke's first trip to his grandparents' home, but Bluebird and White Hawk had made the trip many times before.

Little Fawn and Luke Medicine Horse were happy and excited to have their eldest sister and brother-in-law along, because they didn't see them much, only at Rendezvous or an occasional visit.

While they were traveling, Little Fawn couldn't stop thinking about Caleb Hancock. She couldn't wait to see him again, especially when he would come courting. She herself couldn't explain it, but there was something about him that she liked and she believed that they were meant to be together. However, she wouldn't tell her father that.

Even though Liam O'Reilly was not Bluebird and Little Fawn's real father, they loved and honored him all the same. Ever since he married their mother eight summers previously, he had been nothing but a loving, caring and protective father to them and their brother. There wasn't a thing that he wouldn't do for them and their mother.

"What are you thinking, little sister?" asked Bluebird.

"What makes you think that I am thinking of anything?"

"I know what you're thinking about," said Luke with a mischievous grin.

"And just what I am thinking about, you pesky little mosquito?"

"Caleb!"

Choke Cherry Woman and Bluebird laughed while Liam just shook his head, smiling. "You really do like the lad?" he asked.

Little Fawn just shrugged. "What's there not to like, Father?"

"Take your time, lass," said Liam. "If it is love, then it will keep."

"Sound advice," said Choke Cherry Woman.

As they continued to travel, following the river, Liam was in deep thought. Choke Cherry Woman could sense it. "Something on your mind, husband?"

"Just worried about Azariah and his folks," said Liam. "It is a longer ride from the Arapaho winter camp to their cabin than it is from the Cheyenne's to ours."

Choke Cherry Woman rode up next to him and gently placed her hand on his shoulder. "He Who Walks Tall and

Sweet Grass can take care of themselves," she said. "You know this better than anyone else."

"Aye, I know, but his parents, his sister and her family, they are new to the mountains. A lot can happen."

"We shouldn't worry about what can happen when it is out of our control."

Liam turned to his bride and smirked. "Since when did you get all philosophical?"

Choke Cherry Woman just smiled and said, "The benefits of being married to a good man."

Liam suddenly leaned over and kissed her. White Hawk just smirked, while Bluebird and Little Fawn smiled. Luke Medicine Horse was a different story. "Ewww," he said. "Pa has the cooties!"

Something is wrong with that lad, thought Liam.

9

ENEMIES

About two days after the encounter with the she-grizzly, the Hancock family camped near what is now the border between the states of Colorado and Wyoming. They found a secluded spot near some cottonwoods. Azariah, Jason, Adam, and Caleb went hunting, while Reverend Hancock, Two Hawks, and the boys were bringing in some firewood. By the time the hunters had returned with an antelope, the women had the fire and coffee going.

Azariah and Two Hawks were a little on edge and everyone could sense it. They were traveling through Ute country and about to enter Shoshone country. Both tribes were longtime enemies of the Cheyenne and Arapaho, however, the latter was friendly with most trappers. Azariah had very little to no conflict with the Shoshone people, in fact just the opposite. Shoshone, like most tribes, respected the white giant known as He Who Walks Tall since they knew his reputation as a man of great integrity. The only problem they had with him was that he was an adopted member of the Arapaho Nation and an ally to the Cheyenne and Lakota—all enemies. The Utes were another matter. That tribe and the Arapaho had been hated enemies as long as anyone could remember, and both Azariah and Liam had had run-ins with them. In fact, it was eight years prior that a Ute war party led by four white renegade trappers had kidnapped some Cheyenne women and children from that year's Rendezvous. Choke Cherry Woman and her daughters were among the kidnapped victims. Liam and Azariah led a coalition of Cheyenne and Arapaho warriors to rescue the women and punish the perpetrators, which they successfully did. It was there that Liam met Choke Cherry Woman who was a widow and they became close and eventually fell in love and got married. Azariah remembered the incident as if it were yesterday, because among the kidnapped victims were three Blackfoot girls, who were members of the Kainai clan. He had escorted them back to their people.

The Utes held a long grudge against Azariah since then and many individual Ute warriors came and tried to take his scalp but failed, and it cost them their lives. Azariah was not a violent man, despite his temper. He was usually a man of peace. If he could, he would live in peace with all the tribes. But like many trappers who chose to live among any tribe they marry into, not only do their friends become your friends, but their enemies become your enemies.

Azariah understood this, but he didn't like it. He did find some solace that the Blackfeet and their allies, the Gros Ventre, at least left him and his family alone. The Blackfoot Confederacy were the most dominant tribe of the Northern Plains and they were feared. They mostly traded with the Hudson Bay Fur Company in Canada, but they hated American trappers and any other tribe that wasn't part of their confederacy. While their territories were in what is now northern Montana and southwestern Canada, they were a nomadic tribe and they went wherever they pleased, following the buffalo or raiding other tribes as far south to what is now the state of Utah. They often traveled through the Beartooth Mountains where the Hancock and O'Reilly families made their homes. When He Who Walks Tall returned the three Blackfoot girls back to their people, along with the two ringleaders who kidnapped them, Buffalo Hump, the Kainai Blackfoot chief and father of two of the girls, sent word to other Blackfoot villages that the white giant and his family were to be left in peace. Since then, neither Azariah nor Liam had had any run-ins or encounters with members of the feared Blackfoot Nation, however, the same could not be said for other trappers.

If there was any kind of man that Azariah Hancock truly hated and considered an enemy, it was rapists and child killers, men who preyed on the vulnerable and the weak.

Azariah hated those kinds of men, and it didn't matter what skin color they were or what their lot in life was, he had no mercy for them and for good reason. As he sat down on a log, watching the women cutting up the antelope and putting some of the meat on a spit, his eyes turned to his twin sister, Abigail. Memories of what happened to her sixteen years ago back in Maryland returned. What Belshazzar Jones did to her... She was just fourteen years old. Azariah remembered when he saw the look in Belshazzar's face before he sent him to Hell for what he did to poor Abigail. The man not only bragged about raping her but threatened to do it again and make Azariah watch. What made Azariah even madder was that the son of a bitch didn't even beg for his life, not even after Azariah pulled the trigger on his father's blunderbuss. Belshazzar's dying words and the look on his face was that of a man who had no regrets. That bothered Azariah tremendously. Over the years, as he became a trapper and mountain man, he had tortured and killed many men who were just like Belshazzar Jones. Most of them were other trappers. In fact, Azariah could count the number of Indians he had killed with just one hand.

This was one of the reasons the tribes called him He Who Walks Tall and why he was so respected. While rape was committed by some individual Indian warriors when they raided an enemy village, it was not encouraged, and among many tribes, attacks against women were not tolerated. The fact that more men who were guilty of such heinous crimes had fallen at the hands of He Who Walks Tall was well known among the tribes and among the trapping fraternity, and it was one of the reasons most trappers feared him. However, very few people knew the reason behind his actions.

One who did was the woman who knew him best, Sweet Grass. As she was turning over the meat on the spit, she looked at her husband and sensed that he was troubled. She wasn't alone. Her mother, Clay Basket, was watching him too and took over turning the meat.

"Go to him," was all she said.

Sweet Grass sat next to her husband and watched as he was staring at his sister, Abigail. That's when she knew. She didn't even need to ask.

"It's coming back," said Azariah.

Sweet Grass gently placed her hand on her husband's. "She is safe now," she said. "And she is a lot stronger than you think."

Everyone else was oblivious to Azariah's troubled expression, except Caleb. He saw his uncle and his aunt staring at his mother while talking to each other. Azariah's eyes then fell on Caleb, before he closed them and buried his head in his huge hands. Sweet Grass tried to comfort him, whispering in his ear.

"Are you all right, Uncle?" asked Caleb.

Azariah raised his head and gave a slight smile. "I'm fine," he said. "Just thinking is all."

"I know it has something to do with my mother."

The statement got everyone's attention. Azariah was thinking for a minute and decided that there was no reason to lie to his nephew, but he didn't want Abraham, Jacob, or his own children to know. "Painful memories is all." After he said that, he took Sweet Grass by the hand, got up, and they both went to check on the horses. Both Mother and Sister Abigail could see the sadness in his eyes before he left.

Two Hawks, who was sitting next to Reverend Hancock with the twins, whispered in his ear, "He blames himself for what happened."

"He told you this?"

The Arapaho sub-chief nodded. Reverend Hancock thought for a moment. Adam and Sarah were confused. They knew something was wrong with their father and it had something to do with

their Aunt Abigail, but they didn't know what.

Reverend Hancock, his wife and daughter, along with Caleb followed Azariah and Sweet Grass to where the horses were feeding. Azariah was looking at nothing in particular while rubbing down his horse. He heard his family coming but said nothing.

"We need to talk, son," said Reverend Hancock.

Azariah and Sweet Grass turned around, the former nodding. Azariah looked at Caleb. He could see Abigail's features in him, but he could also see some of Belshazzar's and that made him tense.

"Caleb," he said, "I'm sure you have some questions for me."

Caleb was quiet for a moment before responding. "Actually, I have just one," he asked. "Did that bastard rape my mother?"

Azariah nodded. "But that is not why I killed him."

The reverend, Mother Abigail, and Sister Abigail had questioning looks on their faces.

"I killed him because he would have done it again, and he would have his friends join in," he said. "He threatened to make me watch."

Caleb nodded as if he understood. "Did you know that my mother was pregnant because of it?"

Azariah approached his young nephew. He looked at his sister, who had tears streaming down her cheeks. "Does it matter?"

"No," said Caleb. "I guess it doesn't." At that Caleb hugged Azariah, and his uncle reciprocated.

"Brother," said Sister Abigail, "it wasn't your fault."

"I should've been there to protect you from that animal!"

"That still doesn't mean it was your fault," she said. She approached Azariah, and she could see the tears in his eyes. "You protected me the only way you could have, and that's enough."

"Your sister is right," said their father. "There is no need to punish yourself for what you had no control over." The reverend approached his children and grandson. "God has brought us full circle and we are a family once again." He looked at Sweet Grass and smiled. "He has given you a beautiful and good wife and me and your mother four more beautiful grandchildren added to the three we already have!"

"What more can anyone ask for?" said Mother Abigail as she approached. They wanted to talk to Azariah about his reputation and the men he had killed, but that could wait for another time.

Young Jacob Allen ran out of the camp and shouted, "Dinner is ready!"

As they were returning, Azariah sensed something and turned to see that the horses had stopped eating. Something in the wind had gotten their attention. Azariah scanned the woods to see who or what was there but he saw no movement. Sweet Grass also noticed that something was amiss and placed her hand on one of her pistols in her knife belt. Reverend Hancock noticed their expressions and was also scanning the woods. Azariah, with a turn of his head, signaled his father to get the family back to the camp, whereby the reverend quickly escorted his wife, daughter and grandsons back to camp.

"What is it, husband?" asked Sweet Grass.

"I don't know, but I have a feeling that we are being watched." Azariah had his Hawken rifle and was pointing it towards the south. The forest was quiet. That meant something or someone was in the vicinity. Azariah and Sweet Grass both stood there for at least a minute before the sound of a chipmunk squeaked. Then a couple of blue jays started singing again. Whatever it was, it was gone. Azariah and Sweet Grass turned and both jogged back to camp.

The following morning, the family was back on the trail. Whatever had spooked them the previous night was probably gone, but Azariah was not taking any chances. He talked with Two Hawks, Clay Basket, and Sweet Grass, and it was agreed that they would avoid the river and stay close to the trail as they continued north. They knew they were in Shoshone country, but that didn't mean that they were safe. A roving war party of Utes could still track them, and the scalp of the mighty He Who Walks Tall was too tempting for a Ute warrior to pass up.

Young Adam Hancock, who was growing into a skilled tracker like his uncles, Liam O'Reilly and Howling Wolf, volunteered to lead the small caravan as they traveled up the game trail. His father decided to take the rear and keep a lookout. It was almost the end of August, but it was still summer and grizzly bears were still about. The family had traveled almost ten miles already but it would be another week or two before they reached their cabin in the Beartooth Mountains.

Suddenly the forest went quiet. Adam immediately called a halt by raising his hand in the air. No one said anything as they knew something was amiss, like the night before. Abraham and Jacob were getting scared and stayed close to their parents who quietly comforted them. Azariah,

Jason, Caleb, Two Hawks and even Reverend Hancock had their rifles cocked and ready as they scanned their surroundings. Something or someone was watching them. No one saw any movement. Jason turned around on the saddle to ask Azariah a question, when at that moment an arrow whizzed past his neck, missing it by an inch, harmlessly hit a log. Jason turned in time to see an Indian about to fire another arrow into him before a shot rang and his head exploded like a watermelon.

"Utes!" shouted Azariah who was reloading his rifle.

Jason saw another Indian come at him with a war club and he instinctively raised his rifle and fired without hesitation. The enemy combatant was blasted back by the musket ball at least a few feet before landing on the ground staring at the huge hole in his chest.

"Head for higher ground!" shouted Reverend Hancock who had already dodge a Ute arrow himself, before firing at its owner, hitting him in the stomach.

Adam led them at high speed towards a cul de sac, dodging a rain of arrows in the process. Once they reached it, they put up a defensive position—the women and children stayed with the horses, near the wall, as the men had rifles reloaded and at the ready and stood between them and the oncoming warriors. Azariah counted at least ten Ute warriors, all painted for war, and their bloodlust was up. They knew who he was, because very few white men were as tall and big as he was and they knew he had red hair.

"Make your shots count," was all he said as he aimed his Hawken at the oncoming war party. He singled out who he thought was the leader and fired, knocking him off his horse. Two Hawks, Reverend Hancock, Jason and Caleb followed, and four more of the enemy went down.

The Utes stopped their charge and took cover. There were five left, but they were determined. Mother Abigail had reloaded her husband's rifle as did Clay Basket and Sister Abigail for their husbands. Sweet Grass gave Azariah an extra rifle he always kept that was loaded and ready, while she reloaded his Hawken. Adam and Sarah were armed and stayed by the horses to protect their younger siblings and cousins.

"Which tribe are they?" asked Caleb who had just finished reloading his rifle.

"Utes," said Azariah. "Enemies to the Arapaho and a thorn in my side for a while."

"I was hoping to avoid this," said Reverend Hancock.

Azariah turned to his father. "If you're going to live out here, Father, encounters like these are unavoidable."

His father was about to ask why, when the five remaining Utes fired arrows into the air. "Take cover!" shouted Azariah.

Everyone took cover. Fortunately, all the arrows missed their targets. Young Sarah Sunshine had grabbed her cousin Abraham at the last minute before an arrow landed at the spot he had just occupied.

Suddenly gunshots rang out from behind the Utes and

their number was now reduced to three. The surviving war party immediately noticed that they were being attacked from behind and managed to jump on their horses and hightail it out of there. Not having any time to pick up their dead or wounded, they left them there. A couple of war cries were heard before the Utes left, giving them an incentive to flee and not return.

"What just happened?" asked Jason, who was still watching the retreating Utes.

"We had help," said Azariah. "And I think I know who."

Riders appeared from the north and as they got closer, Azariah, Sweet Grass, Two Hawks and Clay Basket were smiling from ear to ear.

"Uncle Liam!" shouted the twins. "And Aunt Choke Cherry Woman!"

The Irishman and his wife rode their horses until they were at least three feet from their friends. "I can't bloody leave you alone for a second without you getting into some sort of trouble!"

"You're a sight for sore eyes," said Azariah. "How did you know?"

"He was worried about you," said Choke Cherry Woman. "He thought it best that we come and try to meet at the Arapahos' winter camp before you head back home."

"It was blind luck that we found you here instead," said Liam.

"Or Divine Providence," said Reverend Hancock.

"That too," smiled the Irishman.

"Is Little Fawn with you?" asked an anxious Caleb.

Before anyone could answer, Little Fawn rode in, followed by her sister, brother and brother-in-law. Caleb immediately ran to her and helped her off her horse. Without even thinking twice, the two teenagers embraced. Both Liam and Sister Abigail loudly cleared their throats to disrupt the romantic reunion, while their spouses were grinning widely.

10

THE BEARTOOTH MOUNTAINS

After the battle with the Ute war party, Azariah, Liam, Two Hawks, Adam, and White Hawk collected weapons from the dead Ute warriors, while the rest of the two families managed to collect the Ute horses and add them to their caravan. The dead men obviously did not need them.

As Jason and Sister Abigail were bringing one horse, they stopped in horror to find young Adam scalping two of the dead Utes. He wasn't the only one. Azariah, Liam, and White Hawk were taking scalps off the Utes they had killed. Reverend Hancock wasn't surprised, for his son and Two Hawks had explained why scalping was practiced, but it didn't make what he and the rest of the family witnessed any easier. He managed to get Jason and Abigail to keep moving with the horses, while he requested Azariah and Liam not to show their bloody trophies to the children.

Azariah was about to oblige his father, when Adam approached with the scalps of the Utes that his grandfather and Uncle Jason had killed. Both Jason and Abigail thought they might vomit. Azariah told his son to put away the scalps and not show them to anyone. Adam was about to ask why, but his father's look told him to obey and obey he did.

"When the time comes," said Reverend Hancock to Azariah, "we need to talk about your reputation."

Azariah just nodded. He knew his parents did not approve of some of the things he had done, based on the stories they had heard.

About a week after the fight with the Utes, the two families arrived at the foot of the Beartooth Mountains. They were at the borders of what is now the states of northwestern Wyoming and south-central Montana. Liam and Azariah, along with their wives and children, made their homes in a valley near Granite Peak, the highest peak in the Beartooth Mountains.

Liam O'Reilly chose the Beartooth Mountains as his home many years previously because of the remoteness of the region. While the Crow tribe considered the mountains a part of their territory, many tribes traveled through them because the valleys gave excellent protection from blizzards during harsh winters and game was always plentiful.

When the two families arrived in their valley, they were at least ten miles from Granite Peak, which overshadowed their two cabins.

Azariah's family just sat on their horses in dumbstruck awe as they looked at what was part of the majestic Rockies.

"Only in my dreams have I seen such beauty," said Reverend Hancock.

"They make the mountains we have back east look like ant mounds," said Mother Abigail.

"So this is what the Garden of Eden looked like," added Jason.

Azariah turned to his brother-in-law and said, "Even the Garden of Eden had serpents."

"You expecting more trouble?" asked Sister Abigail.

"Always expect trouble, when you live in the wilderness," answered Azariah. "Anything can happen."

"Then why live here if there is so much danger?" asked Caleb.

"Freedom, lad," said Liam as he stretched in his saddle. "Pure and true freedom."

"I don't understand, Mr. O'Reilly," said Caleb.

"In the settlements, what you call civilization," said Liam, "men and women are slaves to rules and regulations created by rich political bloodsuckers who make and break them every day, but out here, a man is free to be who he is and live by his own rules and not by anyone else's."

Azariah's family understood what the Irishman was saying. Civilization had way too many rules that nine times out of ten were created by those in power, who flaunted and lauded them over those who were not.

"I agree with you except for one thing, Mr. O'Reilly," said Reverend Hancock.

"That being?"

"We are not negroes," said the reverend. "If you want to see people who deserve and yearn for true freedom, walk a mile in their shoes."

Liam O'Reilly looked approvingly at the good reverend. "I won't argue with that, for you are correct, but that is what living out here makes even more beautiful—a man, no matter his skin color or his predicament, can live free and not worry about the hypocritical rules that civilized society heaps on them."

"That is what I am afraid of," said Reverend Hancock.

"What do you mean?" Liam replied.

"Father believes trouble will soon come to the tribes," said Azariah. "In the form of more white people coming west to settle."

Liam thought for a moment and believed the reverend was right about that. "That bothers you, Reverend?"

"It does... and it should bother you and Azariah," answered Reverend Hancock. "You both have lived peacefully with the Arapaho and Cheyenne and many tribes who respect you, I fear as more whites come, more trouble follows."

"It might not happen in our time, White Medicine Eagle," said Two Hawks.

"White Medicine Eagle?" questioned Liam.

"That is the name we have given him, Raging Bull," said Two Hawks. "We shouldn't worry about what will happen tomorrow or in our children's children's time, especially if we have no control over it."

"Two Hawks is right," Liam agreed. "We can only worry about and control what happens right now and let tomorrow take care of itself."

Azariah knew his father-in-law and best friend were correct, but he shared his father's concern. He, like Liam, was loyal to the Arapaho and Cheyenne Nations, and if the nightmare that his father had was a small glimpse of the future, he wondered whether it could be changed and prevented from happening. Worse, was it meant not to be changed but endured?

11

COURTSHIP

The families arrived at the Hancocks' cabin about less than a day later. The O'Reillys' cabin was three miles north, but the Irishman and his family decided to stay with Azariah's family for the time being to give the horses time to rest. The tipis were set up in no time and because there wasn't enough room for Azariah's parents and his sister's family to stay in the cabin, it was decided that they would stay in their own tipis that were made for them before they left the Arapaho winter encampment.

Azariah and Sweet Grass went to check the inside of their home to make sure they didn't have any visitors, either four-legged or two-legged, and were relieved to find that their cabin had been unmolested during the time they were gone. The women immediately got to work cleaning the cabin of dust, while Azariah and Adam went to check the smokehouse. Meat was needed, so it was decided that the men would go hunting the next morning. They were happy to be home.

Later that evening at dinner, stories were told by Azariah's parents about what has been going on back in the east over the past sixteen years, from the election of John Quincy Adams to the election of Andrew Jackson (who Mother Abigail called the Devil incarnate because of his anti-Indian policies.) The family even talked about the Nat Turner insurrection and its aftermath. What Azariah was most interested in Belshazzar Jones' father and uncle who had bounties on his head.

"I wouldn't worry about them," said Jason. "Frederick Jones drank himself to death back in '26 and his brother was assassinated back in '32."

"Looks like there is justice after all," said Azariah.

"What is assassinated?" asked Sweet Grass. While she knew and spoke English, she didn't understand all the white man's words.

"It's another word for murder or to kill," answered Reverend Hancock.

"Why do you white men use big words?" asked Choke Cherry Woman.

Reverend Hancock just laughed and shrugged. He agreed with Choke Cherry Woman's assessment of his kind and he wasn't alone. Liam and Azariah thought that men of their kind were too high falutin' for their own good.

After dinner, Caleb thought he needed a bath. Fortunately, there was a lake not far from the cabin but it was getting dark, so he decided to head down to take a dip. Azariah had warned him to be aware of his surroundings and keep his weapons close by. Caleb listened as he left, carrying his weapons, along with a bar of soap that he brought from the settlements. After he undressed and slowly walked into the water, he felt its cool moisture with his feet before going farther into the lake. Caleb had never been much for skinny dipping, mainly because he was self-conscious about his body. While he was not muscular by any means, he wasn't fat either. He was also shy around women, which is why his feelings for Little Fawn surprised his parents. He had never shown any interest in the opposite sex, which concerned his stepfather up until now.

Caleb was just thinking about what attracted him to Little Fawn, when he inadvertently turned around and found her coming towards him, completely naked. The young man's eyes nearly bulged out of his sockets as he tried to regain his composure but he slipped and fell backwards, dropping the soap while submerged. As he resurfaced, he found Little Fawn giggling at him. This time, she was much closer to him than before.

"Little Fawn," he spluttered, "you shouldn't be here!"

"Why?" she asked innocently.

"Because if your father sees us like this, he will kill me, that's why!"

"No, he won't," said Little Fawn.

Caleb was grateful that her breasts were submerged because he already had an erection that he wasn't sure he could get rid of. He turned around and submerged himself to find his soap and managed to find it before resurfacing. She was still standing before him, and he couldn't help but notice how beautiful she was. Granted, they had been courting for a while, but this was the first time he had seen her naked, and he had a feeling of both excitement and doom.

Little Fawn noticed the soap in his hand and asked, "Is that what you white men clean yourselves with?"

Caleb sheepishly nodded. "I used to watch my parents clean each other's backs every time they bathed."

She approached him and gently took the soap from him. Caleb slowly turned around and allowed her to scrub his back with the lye soap as he covered his submerged manhood with his hands. Her touch felt angelic to him as he allowed himself to relax a bit.

When she was done, she washed off the soap and turned him around towards her. "Can you wash my back?" she asked.

Before Caleb could oblige, a look of horror appeared on his face as he was staring past her.

"You touch her and I will turn your head into a bloody canoe!" shouted Liam O'Reilly, armed with his Hawken rifle.

Not long later, the two love-struck teenagers were inside the cabin, standing before their parents.

"Caleb Nehemiah Hancock!" shouted Sister Abigail. "I am so surprised at you!" She was about as angry at her son as Liam was. Her husband was another matter, though.

"So am I," he said with a smile. "For a minute there, you had me worried, you lucky little devil, you!"

"Jason, be serious," scolded Abigail.

"I would listen to your wife if I were you," said a very angry Liam. "If Caleb were anyone else, I would have killed him for attempting to violate my daughter!"

"Now, that is a very serious accusation, Mr. O'Reilly," said Jason. "Caleb could never do such a thing!"

"Father, Caleb did not do anything that I didn't want him to do," said Little Fawn.

"See?" said Jason.

Little Fawn added, "If anything, I was trying to violate *him*."

Both Liam and Sister Abigail's bottom lips hit the floor, Choke Cherry Woman had to stifle a chuckle, while Jason guffawed as he patted Caleb on the back, who by this time was blushing red.

Choke Cherry Woman managed to calm everyone down a bit, especially after Little Fawn explained that all she and Caleb were doing was taking a bath. Nothing more was happening or going to happen. Abigail thought that maybe the two should take a break from courting, but Jason convinced her that she was overreacting and that the two teenagers were good for each other. Choke Cherry Woman agreed. Liam was inclined to agree with Caleb's mother but decided to compromise and said that the lad could continue to court his daughter on the condition that there would be no more bathing or skinny dipping. The two teenagers agreed and that was that.

Azariah, Sweet Grass and the rest of the party were outside listening, when Liam exited the cabin. "So how did it go?" asked Azariah.

"The lad is lucky that he is your nephew," retorted Liam as he stormed off.

Choke Cherry Woman just smiled and shook her head. "He will calm down," she said. "You know how overprotective he is."

Azariah just nodded. "I fear the day when my daughters become teenagers."

"What are you going to do, husband?" asked Sweet Grass. "Strangle the first suitor that comes calling?"

"Exactly!"

12

UNWELCOME VISITORS

The next morning, the women and children went down to the lake to take a bath. It took a while for both Mother and Sister Abigail as well as Abraham and Jacob to overcome their shyness. They had never bathed together before or with other people. But once they were in the water, they relaxed and it wasn't before long Jacob was splashing water at his brother and Luke. When Sister Abigail tried to scold them, they splashed her, and before long everybody was joining in on the fun.

"Now that looks like fun," said a voice from the bank.

The women and children stopped their play and turned their attention to the source of the voice and found six men on horseback. One white man, who appeared to be in his late forties to early fifties, and five Indians who appeared to be much younger.

"You!" shouted Choke Cherry Woman as she recognized the white man.

"Why, hello, Mrs. O'Reilly," said the white man in a thick Scottish brogue.

"What are you doing here, MacAnnish?"

"Now, last time I checked, this was Crow country, so I should be asking you that question."

"Who is this riffraff?" asked Mother Abigail.

"Samuel MacAnnish," answered Choke Cherry Woman. "He is a murderer!"

"No more than your jackass of a husband and his friend He Who Walks Tall," said MacAnnish. "Where are those two anyway?"

"Right behind you, MacAnnish," said Liam. "You and your sons keep your hands where we can see them or you will find yourselves in Hell real quick!"

"You would shoot a man and his sons in the back, wouldn't you?" said MacAnnish.

"A man like you? Absolutely," responded Liam.

"Is that how it was with my brother?"

"Your brother had it coming!" shouted Azariah.

The Scotsman suddenly chuckled. "Azariah Hancock, I figured you would be here."

"Pa," said Azariah to his father, "you and Jason get the women and children out of here. We'll cover you."

Nehemiah and Jason quickly walked past Samuel MacAnnish and his five sons to escort their loved ones away from them. As the women and children quickly got dressed, Jason noticed that one of MacAnnish's sons was staring at Abigail lustfully. Without hesitation, Jason ran up to the man, who appeared to be MacAnnish's eldest son, and pulled him off his horse. The Indian hit the ground hard, but quickly recovered and was about to reach for his knife when he found himself staring down the barrel of Jason's Hawken rifle.

"Please," said Jason. "Give me an excuse."

"Bloody hell!" shouted MacAnnish. "What right did you have to do that to me son?"

"Your son should learn not to look at another man's wife!"

"Time for you and your boys to leave, MacAnnish," said Liam.

MacAnnish turned to his son, who was slowly getting up on his feet and staring at Jason with pure hatred in his eyes. "Easy, Jericho. Can you ride?"

"Yeah, I can ride," said Jericho MacAnnish. He managed to slowly retrieve his rifle and mounted his horse, while not taking his eyes off Jason, who still had his own Hawken on him.

"I won't forget this, O'Reilly," said Samuel MacAnnish.

"I'm sure," responded Liam.

"Let's ride," said Samuel MacAnnish in the Crow tongue as he and his sons slowly rode away.

Azariah and Liam told Nehemiah and Jason to take the women and children back to their cabin, while they followed the MacAnnish men to make sure that they left their valley.

"What did he mean when he said, 'Was it the same for his brother?'" asked Mother Abigail to Choke Cherry Woman.

"Liam killed Samuel MacAnnish's older brother two years ago."

"I'm sure he had a good reason," said Jason.

"He did," said Sweet Grass. "His brother tried to rape a ten-year-old girl, The only way to stop him was to kill him."

13

BLOOD FEUD

Samuel MacAnnish and his older brother, Hamish, had come to America from Scotland in 1800, when they were in their late teens. Hamish had an issue of not keeping his pants zipped and that got him in hot water back in their hometown of Inverness. Samuel had often looked up to his older brother, so when Hamish was forced to leave home for violating a wealthy landowner's daughter, Samuel went with him. Their journey took them to St. Louis where they signed up with some free trappers, most of them French Canadians, and they ended up trading and living with the Crow tribe. While Hamish could never settle down with any one woman, Samuel did fall in love and married the daughter of a Crow medicine man. She would be the mother of his five sons: Jericho, Ahab, Cain, Pharoah and Saul.

While the Crow mostly tolerated and respected Samuel, they didn't think too highly of his brother. So Hamish would often travel and open trade with other tribes such as the Shoshone, Flathead, Nez Perce and Ute, but he would always come back and visit the Crow just to be near his younger brother and nephews. His history of violence towards women, especially young women, finally caught up to him at the 1834 Rendezvous, when he attacked a ten-year-old Cheyenne girl. However, before he had the chance to fully rape her, Liam O'Reilly came from behind him and blew out his brains, sending him straight to Hell.

Samuel MacAnnish never forgave the white man known as Raging Bull for killing his elder brother, even though he was in the wrong. Despite the fact that the Crow and Cheyenne tribes were mortal enemies, and Samuel was Crow by both marriage and adoption, not many Crows who knew the MacAnnish family were going to lose sleep over the death of Hamish MacAnnish. Since the incident happened at Rendezvous, which was considered neutral territory, everyone believed that Liam was in the right. Once the Cheyenne girl testified to those in charge at Rendezvous regarding what Hamish MacAnnish tried to do to her, it was clear that the killing was justified and there would be no repercussions against Liam O'Reilly.

However, his actions did start a blood feud between him and Samuel MacAnnish and his family. Samuel and his three oldest sons were close to his brother, despite that he was a deviant. They wanted revenge against O'Reilly and the Cheyenne. Not long after the death of Hamish, some individual Cheyenne warriors suddenly disappeared while hunting. Their bodies were later found scalped and mutilated. Both Liam and Azariah suspected the MacAnnish men behind the killings, but without proof, they couldn't retaliate.

That changed in the fall of 1835, when Samuel and his sons, along with his brother-in-law, Heavy Eagle, joined a Crow war party expedition that the latter led against the Cheyenne. The raid was a disaster, and Heavy Eagle was killed by a Cheyenne arrow. Jericho MacAnnish witnessed who killed his maternal uncle and it was none other than Thunder Cloud, Liam O'Reilly's brother-in-law from his first marriage.

Having lost two uncles, one from each side of his family, Jericho MacAnnish hated the white man called Raging Bull and the Cheyenne just as much as his father did. Both father and son vowed to get even. They were hateful and hotheaded but they were not fools.

Like many Indians and trappers who had heard of Liam O'Reilly and knew his reputation, they also knew that where he was, the white giant known as He Who Walks Tall was not far behind. As they traveled out of the valley, Samuel MacAnnish was putting his plan into motion.

"What are we going to do, Pa?" asked Jericho.

"About what?"

"About Raging Bull."

"Nothing as of now," said Samuel.

"Nothing," said Ahab in a tone louder than he meant to. "Uncle Hamish and Uncle Heavy Eagle are both dead because of that son of a bitch!"

Samuel turned and looked at his second eldest dead in the eye. "No one has more reason to see Raging Bull dead more than me," he said. "But we need to think."

"About what?" asked Jericho. His blood lust was up. He not only wanted to kill Liam O'Reilly, he also wanted to kill that other white man named Jason Allen for humiliating him.

"O'Reilly is not alone," said Samuel. "Azariah Hancock is with him and he, like his Irish buddy, are trained killers."

"So are we," said Ahab. "He Who Walks Tall doesn't frighten me."

Samuel almost laughed, not in mockery, but with a little pride in his son. "There is a difference between not being afraid and being foolish," he said. "He Who Walks Tall can break you in half with just a bear hug."

"At least we now know where they live," said Jericho.

"Absolutely, son," added Samuel with a wicked smile. "Now we know."

"We're asking for a lot of trouble, I think," said Saul. The youngest of Samuel MacAnnish's five sons, the sixteen-year-old Saul was more level-headed than his father and older brothers and had not been as close to his Uncle Hamish. Neither was Pharaoh. Both had witnessed their uncle's perversions while on raids against enemy tribes, but they would never say anything about it, because he was family.

"Oh, you do?" remarked Samuel. He always felt that his two youngest sons weren't as strong as their brothers and were weak. They didn't always agree with their father's actions. "Have you forgotten what Raging Bull did to your uncle?" he asked angrily. "Or how about your Uncle Heavy Eagle, killed by one of Raging Bull's family members!"

"Uncle Heavy Eagle was killed in battle, Pa," said Pharaoh. "As far as Uncle Hamish is concerned, I heard he had it coming."

Samuel backhanded his son in the mouth. Saul wanted to come to his brother's aid, but he was afraid of their father. Samuel was about to do more damage, but Jericho and Ahab intervened.

"He didn't mean it, Pa," said Jericho. "Did you, Pharaoh?"

The seventeen-year-old just slowly shook his head and apologized as he wiped the small amount of blood from his lip.

"What the bloody hell is wrong with you two anyway?" said Samuel to both Pharaoh and Saul. "Why can't you be like your brothers? I mean, hell, even your mother hates Raging Bull and the Cheyenne."

Cain, who was the quietest of the bunch, almost snickered. *She wasn't too fond of Uncle Hamish, either,* he thought to himself.

"So how do you want to deal with Raging Bull and He Who Walks Tall, Father?" asked Ahab in Crow.

Samuel gave a wicked smile. "By hitting them where it hurts!"

14

KIDNAPPED

A couple of days later at the Hancock cabin, it had been uneventful since the encounter with the MacAnnish men. The O'Reilly family had returned to their home three miles north and his kin, but they promised they would be back to help build cabins for Azariah's parents and his sister's family. Liam O'Reilly had always been a man of his word. It was one of the reasons Choke Cherry Woman loved him so much. He reminded her of her first husband who was the same way. His death was hard on her and their daughters, but he would never have wanted her to remain a widow and mourn him.

Liam filled his moccasins and then some and had become an excellent father to Bluebird and Little Fawn. Maybe a little overprotective, but what father wasn't? He also never played favorites. Even after Luke Medicine Horse was born, Liam made sure all his children were loved equally. If anything, he and Choke Cherry Woman doted on their grandson, Spotted Bear. Every time they visited their Cheyenne relatives, the grandparents were always eager to see their first and only grandchild. Bluebird often scolded her parents for spoiling the little tyke to which her father would respond, "That is what grandparents do!"

While riding to visit the Hancock family, Liam was on edge. He wasn't the only one. Choke Cherry Woman knew her husband well and sensed that he was worried and suspicious that Samuel MacAnnish and his sons were still in the area, watching and plotting. However, they both kept quiet about it until they reached Azariah and Sweet Grass' home.

Seeing their Uncle Liam and Aunt Choke Cherry Woman again was pure joy for young Abigail Little Flower and Solomon White Wolf. Even Abraham and Jacob started calling them Aunt and Uncle, even though they were not even related. When the O'Reilly's arrived, Azariah and Two Hawks were showing Caleb, Abraham, and Jacob how an Arapaho warrior rides a horse, whether in battle or on a hunt and without a saddle. Abigail's boys were learning quickly. Although Jacob was having the hardest time, he never gave up.

Liam was impressed that the families had started building the cabins and was going to offer his helping hand, but not before he shared his concerns about the MacAnnish family possibly still being in the area.

"How far do you think he will take it?" asked Reverend Hancock.

Both Azariah and Liam just shrugged. "With Samuel MacAnnish, you never know," said Azariah. "He was very close to his brother obviously, despite the fact that Liam was justified in killing him."

"I don't think we should take any chances," said Liam. "He will try something, and I fear the most vulnerable among us will get caught in the crossfire."

Both Mother and Sister Abigail, and even Jason, were a little surprised. "He wouldn't dare," said Jason. "The man is a father himself."

"Your point?" responded Azariah. "You have met his sons, especially the eldest who looked at my sister the wrong way."

Reverend Hancock for once didn't disagree. "I saw how he looked at you, Jason, after you defended Abigail's honor," he said. "He strikes me as a man who has no limits when it comes to his pride."

Two Hawks offered his opinion. "A man like that will never be satisfied," he said. "When he is full of vengeance, his heart becomes that of stone and he knows no boundaries."

"We can't wait for him to come after us," said Azariah.

"You mean I can't wait for him," said Liam. "It's me he wants to kill and I have to face him."

"Not by yourself, you're not!" insisted Azariah.

"This isn't your fight, He Who Walks Tall."

"How can you say that to me, after all that we have been through together?" said Azariah.

Choke Cherry Woman and Sweet Grass agreed, but before anyone could say anything, Abraham and Jacob were running towards the adults, screaming. Jason and Abigail ran to them.

"Boys, what happened?" asked Abigail.

"We were watching Caleb and Little Fawn walking down by the lake," said Abraham, "when that man, Mac-what's-his-name showed up!"

"He and his sons took them at gunpoint," added Jacob. "We hid, but Luke ran to stop them and they grabbed him too!"

Both Liam and Azariah were on their feet. "Which way did they go?" shouted Liam in a tone that he didn't mean towards the boys. The boys pointed north.

"We're going after them," said Azariah.

"It could be a trap," said Two Hawks. "Remember, MacAnnish is an adopted Crow, and they could be with him to lure you away."

"Which is why only I am going," said Liam.

"Like hell you are!" shouted Azariah. "We are in this together!"

"I'm coming, too," said Jason.

Azariah shook his head and said, "You and Pa need to stay and protect the rest of the family."

"That wasn't a request," said Jason angrily. "Those

bastards have my son and possibly my future daughter-in-law. You want to stop me from coming, then shoot me!"

Both Liam and Azariah were about to say more, but Reverend Hancock and Two Hawks settled it. "You will need all the help you can get," said Two Hawks. "We can take care of the children, and the women as you know are fighters and can take care of themselves."

"That settles it then," said Liam. "Let's mount up. They can't have gone far."

"Wait!" shouted Reverend Hancock. "You do whatever it takes to bring our children home. If that means killing Samuel MacAnnish and his whole brood, then you bury the entire family!"

"Don't you worry about that, Pa," said Azariah. "We will bring them home, come hell or highwater, and MacAnnish will pay!"

15

THIN LINE BETWEEN JUSTICE AND VENGEANCE

The MacAnnish men were riding north, fast, with their quarry. Caleb had been knocked unconscious and was hanging upside down on his horse with both his arms and legs tied to the saddle. Little Fawn and Luke Medicine Horse were bound and gagged and threatened by the MacAnnish patriarch that if they gave them trouble, it would be the last thing they did. Both children of Raging Bull and Choke Cherry put on a brave front, staring straight ahead and showing no fear, even though deep down they were both terrified.

Little Fawn had been through this before and she knew what her captors had in store. She, her brother, and Caleb were bait. Samuel MacAnnish wanted her father. But she was more concerned about the MacAnnish boys, especially

Jericho and Ahab, who both looked at her lustfully. It was a good thing that Liam hadn't found them yet, or that Caleb wasn't awake. They both would have skinned the two alive or died trying. Little Fawn looked at poor Caleb as he bounced around unconscious on his horse. Even if he were awake, there was little he could do. Yes, the children were bait, because the MacAnnish men were deliberately leaving a trail. They wanted Liam O'Reilly and Azariah Hancock and whoever was with them to follow. The question on Little Fawn's mind was would her father and uncle take the bait and walk into a trap?

———

"Samuel MacAnnish is no fool," said Liam. "He and his boys are deliberately leaving a trail for us to follow."

"So we could be riding into a trap," said Jason. "Any ideas?"

The Irishman just shrugged. "For now, we follow," he said. "But it is clear that the children are bait."

"If they harm a hair on Caleb's head..." said Jason angrily.

Azariah managed to calm down his brother-in-law. "Don't think like that," he said. "We will get them back safe and sound."

Jason looked at Liam and then felt ashamed. "I am sorry, Liam. I forgot that they have your children too."

"No need for an apology," said Liam. "I feel the same way."

"Then, it is clear what must be done when we catch up to those bastards?"

Azariah looked at his brother-in-law. "Jason, have you ever killed a man?" he asked. "I mean, up close and personal."

"Why do you ask me that?" asked Jason. "You saw me help fight off those Ute warriors that attacked us."

"This is different," said Azariah. "This is more personal."

"There is a thin line between justice and vengeance," said Liam. "Out here they are one in the same."

"Are you ready for that?" asked Azariah.

"If it means bringing Caleb, Little Fawn, and Luke home safe and sound, then yes, I am ready for it."

"Then let's ride," said Liam. "They couldn't have gone far and I have a plan."

————

Samuel MacAnnish and his sons stopped at a clearing, where a creek was flowing through it. "This is it, boys," said the Scotsman. "This is where we lay our trap."

Jericho and Ahab pulled a now-conscious Caleb off his horse and dragged him, not too gently, to a log near the creek. Little Fawn and Luke Medicine Horse watched helplessly as the two youngest MacAnnish boys, Pharoah and Saul, attempted to gently get the brother and sister down off their mounts. Cain was getting annoyed with his brothers' gentle demeanor towards their prisoners and pushed them out of the way. He grabbed Little Fawn by the hair and threw her to the ground and repeated the process with Luke.

"Was that necessary?" asked Saul.

Cain glared at his youngest brother, ignoring his question, and forced both Little Fawn and Luke to walk to where Caleb was now sitting. Jericho tied their legs together and warned them that if they made a sound, they were dead. The children nodded understanding and their gags were removed.

"You're awfully pretty for a Cheyenne," said Jericho. "It's a shame we don't have time, otherwise I would show you what a real man is."

Little Fawn spat in his face, which caught him off guard.

"You bitch!" Jericho took out his knife and was about to stab Little Fawn but his father intervened.

"No time for that now, son," said Samuel. "After we avenge your uncle, and kill the rest of her family, you and your brothers can do with her as you please."

Pharaoh and Saul didn't like the sound of that. In fact, they felt this had gone on far enough, but they didn't know what to do. They didn't want to go against their own flesh and blood, but this was wrong and they knew it. There was little they could do, wasn't there?

The two youngest MacAnnish boys were looking at each other as if reading each other's minds, but they had to act fast.

"You two," said Samuel, pointing at Pharaoh and Saul.

"Go back and check our backtrail. Let us know if our prey is coming, and I don't need to tell you two to be careful."

"Sure thing, Pa," said Pharaoh.

He and Saul mounted and rode down the backtrail. When they were out of earshot of their father and brothers, they decided what they were going to do.

16

SHOWDOWN

Liam, Azariah and Jason were a mile out from their pursuers, when Pharaoh and Saul MacAnnish appeared from the bushes before them. Each had a white flag hanging from their rifle. It was clear to the trio that they wanted to talk, but they would not let down their guard. They slowly rode up to the MacAnnish boys and stopped about ten feet from them.

"You're riding into a trap, Raging Bull," said Pharaoh, using Liam's Indian name.

"We figured that out."

"We want no part of this," said Saul. "We know that you killing our Uncle Hamish was just."

"Your father and brothers disagree," said Liam. "My question is... why should we trust you?"

"Because we can help you get your children back," said Pharoah. "That's if you want our help."

"We will not come between you and your father," said Azariah. "Just tell us what they have in mind and head back to Crow country."

"I assume that you won't offer our brothers mercy," said Pharaoh.

"From what we could tell, they wouldn't accept," said Liam.

"Will you at least try?" pleaded Saul. "For our mother's sake?"

"We can't make any promises," said Liam.

"You two should consider yourselves lucky that we don't kill *you*," said Jason.

"Easy, Jason," said Azariah.

"Well, lads..." said Liam, "you going to tell us what your father and brothers have in store for us or not?"

"The choice is yours," said Azariah.

Pharoah and Saul looked at each other and shrugged. They told the trio their father's plan and after that, they left the area and headed north towards the Crow village they grew up in.

————

From their hiding positions, Samuel MacAnnish and his three oldest sons were wondering what was taking Pharoah and Saul.

"Those two imbecile brothers of yours should have been back by now to let us know what's going on," said Samuel.

"Maybe Raging Bull and He Who Walks Tall surprised them and killed them," said Jericho.

"Not likely," said his father. "I know Raging Bull. To him they would be just boys, and he would try to convince them that it would be in their best interest to flap their gums about our plans first."

"What about He Who Walks Tall?" asked Ahab. "That son of a bitch was born to end lives, and we have his nephew there along with Raging Bull's two brats!"

Samuel didn't like it. The forest surrounding the opening and creek was too quiet. Something was amiss.

"You should have sent me instead, Father," said Cain. "You can't trust Pharaoh and Saul. They're too weak."

"But at least they are better men than you four bastards!" shouted Liam from behind a tree twenty feet above them.

"Any of you make a move, and you will find yourselves in Hell real quick," shouted Azariah from his hidden position.

Jason was hiding from his position, holding a bead on Jericho MacAnnish, while at the same time watching the children tied together next to a log near the creek in the clearing. He knew that at this moment there was nothing he could do but make sure the MacAnnish boys didn't make a move. He was at least relieved that the children were alive and unharmed. He, Azariah, and Liam were spread out at least thirty feet from each other in their hiding positions behind the MacAnnish men. Samuel MacAnnish knew the trio had the high ground, and he and his boys were trapped. He knew who to blame.

"Tell me, O'Reilly," he said, "you kill Pharaoh and Saul?"

"Nope," said Liam. "They came to us under a flag of truce and told us everything what you had in store for me and my family."

The Scotsman cussed in Gaelic, while his oldest sons cussed in Crow. "I always knew those two were weak," Samuel muttered. "Out of all my brood!"

"It doesn't have to end like this, Samuel," said Liam. "If you want vengeance for your brother, then we settle it the Indian way."

"You mean one on one?"

"Aye," said Liam. "I give you my word that no one on my end will interfere, and Jericho, Ahab and Cain, you three can follow your brothers back to the Crow village."

The Scotsman and his sons laughed maniacally. "You can go straight to hell, Raging Bull!" shouted Jericho. "But I think I will send your brats there first!" Jericho MacAnnish turned and aimed his rifle at the children.

He didn't get the chance to pull the trigger. Jason's Hawken rifle shot true and put a gaping hole in Jericho's chest. The half-Scot, half-Crow immediately dropped his rifle to look at the new hole before collapsing face-first.

Once Jason's shot was fired, all hell broke loose. Samuel MacAnnish and his two surviving sons fired in all directions and made a break for it. But only Ahab MacAnnish didn't make it far. He attempted to head toward the children, but he only reached three feet before his head exploded like a watermelon, courtesy of Azariah's Hawken rifle. That left Samuel and Cain, and they went in different directions to God knows where. Jason slowly and cautiously came from his hiding place and walked to the clearing where the children were held. He untied Little Fawn and Luke Medicine Horse first, removing their gags, before freeing Caleb. He was startled when Azariah appeared from behind, approaching with their horses.

"You kids all right?" asked Jason.

All three nodded, despite the black eye Caleb had. "My noggin is hurting a little bit," he said. "But I don't think it is serious."

"I am relieved to hear that, son," said Jason. "And so will your mother." Jason hugged his stepson.

"Where is father?" asked Little Fawn.

"He is probably taking care of Samuel and Cain MacAnnish," said Azariah.

"Not by himself!" shouted a worried Little Fawn.

"Don't worry, Little Fawn," said Azariah. "Your father can take care of himself."

"Right now," said Jason, "we need to get you kids back home safe and sound."

At that moment, Cain MacAnnish appeared before them. He was armed only with a knife and a Crow war club. "He

Who Walks Tall!" he shouted. "I challenge you to a fight to the death."

"In a minute," said Azariah. He turned towards Jason. "Get the children out of here. They don't need to see what is about to happen."

"What if his father interferes before Liam catches him?" asked Jason.

"He won't," assured Azariah. "Cain MacAnnish sees himself as a Crow warrior rather than a Scotsman, so this is a matter of pure honor." Azariah put down his rifle and took out his Arkansas toothpick and Arapaho tomahawk. "Now, get," he said before returning his attention to Cain.

He approached the young MacAnnish boy who appeared to be no older than twenty. Azariah thought he was throwing his life away. "It doesn't have to be this way, Cain."

Cain laughed. "I am a Crow warrior. My Crow name is Dog Killer," he boasted. "I have counted five coups in my young life and taken three scalps from my enemies, and I will gladly add your scalps to my collection!"

"Many have tried to take my scalp," said Azariah. "All have failed."

"I know of your reputation, He Who Walks Tall," said Cain. "You may be bigger than me and have strong medicine, but I do not fear you!"

"And why is that, Dog Killer?"

"Because I am not weak like my younger brothers who betrayed their family!"

"Or maybe you don't have a conscience like they do," said Azariah.

"At least their conscience was clear, which makes them better men. More than I can say for you and your father."

Cain screamed a war cry and charged. Azariah, who was taller than him by a foot and a half and outweighed him by two hundred pounds, quickly sidestepped him and struck him in the back of the head with the flat side of his tomahawk. The force from the blow knocked the younger man off balance and he tripped over his own two feet in the process, falling face-first. When he got up, he was madder than a she-grizzly that got her cubs stolen.

Azariah Hancock, standing with his knife in his left hand and his tomahawk in his right, just stood and shook his head as if this was his final warning to the young MacAnnish. "You cannot win this," he said.

"Today is a good day to die," said Cain before charging again.

The young MacAnnish struck out with his club, which Azariah blocked with his tomahawk. Cain attempted to stab Azariah with his knife, but missed the taller, larger man's stomach by an inch; however, Azariah managed to jab his Arkansas toothpick into Cain's ribs not once but twice before cutting a huge slash across his abdomen. A shocked Cain took a step back as he watched his insides spill out in front of him. Knowing the end was near, Cain MacAnnish, Dog Killer, sang his death song. Knowing what must be done,

Azariah buried his tomahawk into Cain's skull, killing him instantly.

"You're going to bloody pay for that," growled Samuel MacAnnish. The Scotsman came out of the bushes, pointing his loaded musket at Azariah.

"There has been enough bloodshed, MacAnnish."

"Not for me, there hasn't," said the Scotsman.

"I gave your son every chance not to have it end like this," said Azariah. "He chose to die like a Crow warrior."

"That will give his poor mother and me little comfort," said Samuel.

"Unlike your wife, who will have no comfort at all, since she is soon to be a widow."

"Drop it, MacAnnish," said Liam from out of the shadows. "Azariah is right. There has been enough bloodshed."

"So you just expect me to walk away and forget all this?"

"Aye."

"Not a chance, you dumb Irish bastard!"

Those were the last words of Samuel MacAnnish before he turned and attempted to fire in Liam's direction. The Irishman beat him to it by firing his Hawken, the bullet finding its mark in the Scotsman's belly. Samuel MacAnnish collapsed, face first on the ground. Azariah walked up to him and turned him over and watched as the blood spurted profusely out his stomach. He was convulsing rapidly, but no one died quickly from being gut shot. As Azariah was deciding what to do, Liam appeared beside him and decided to end MacAnnish's misery by cutting his throat.

"He wasn't always like this," said Liam. "He was a good man at one point in his life."

"He must have really loved his brother," said Azariah. "Even if he was not a very good person."

"That is the trouble with this world, my friend," said Liam. "You can pick your friends, but you can't pick your family."

17

A NEW BEGINNING

Two days later, in the Crow village of Big Foot, Pharoah and Saul MacAnnish were helping their mother, Elk Woman, with chores when Liam O'Reilly and Azariah Hancock rode into their village with the bodies of their father and brothers strapped to their horses. The two youngest MacAnnish boys had informed their mother and their chief of what their father and older brothers had done and why they had betrayed them. From their explanation, the whole village expected two things to happen. That Samuel MacAnnish would attempt to avenge his evil brother; and that he and his sons would return with the scalps of Raging Bull and He Who Walks Tall or they wouldn't return at all. No one expected Raging and He Who Walks Tall, their longtime enemies, to show up in their village.

The arrival of the two white men caused some excitement

among the warriors and villagers. Led by Chief Big Foot himself, the warriors surrounded Liam and Azariah, waiting and ready to kill them if ordered. However, it was clear to the chief that the two arrivals didn't come for a fight. The crowd cleared a path, allowing Pharaoh and Saul MacAnnish, along with their mother, to approach.

"We have come to return the bodies of Samuel MacAnnish and his sons to their family," said Liam, using sign language. "We have also come to make peace with the Crow people."

"And why should we accept your offer of peace?" asked Chief Big Foot. "You kill our brother and his sons. What makes you think we won't kill you?"

"I did not want this to happen or end this way," said Liam. "Did not the two youngest sons of MacAnnish tell you what happened?"

The chief turned to Pharaoh and Saul, who just nodded, before he returned his focus back to Liam and nodded.

Before anyone could continue, Elk Woman approached the horses carrying the bodies of her husband and three oldest sons. None of the bodies were scalped and they were wrapped in either white cloths or buffalo robes. She touched each of her sons' bodies, before stopping to touch that of her husband. While Samuel MacAnnish was a hard man to deal with, he was always a good husband, a good father, and a friend when he needed to be. The trouble was his brother. Elk Woman, as most of her people, did not like her brother-in-law, mainly because of his lust and violence towards young girls. While he never committed any such crimes towards Crow girls, young women of other tribes were fair game to him. No one could believe that he was even Samuel's brother, because Samuel was the exact opposite of him. Elk Woman always thought her brother-in-law was an evil influence on her sons, and she did her best to keep them away from him, but at the same time she didn't want to hurt her husband, whose Crow name was White Otter. When she heard that Raging Bull had killed her husband's brother, for attempting to rape a Cheyenne girl at the white man's Rendezvous two summers previously, she was relieved, but that was when her husband changed. He wanted revenge against Raging Bull so badly, it consumed him. Now it had cost him his life and the lives of three of his eldest sons.

"I am sorry, ma'am," said Liam. He never knew Elk Woman's name, nor did he know if she spoke English, but he expected Pharaoh and Saul to translate his apology to their mother. Elk Woman turned her attention to Liam and stared into his eyes, while he sat on his horse. She could see sorrow, but something else as well. She saw that he understood her pain and what she was going through. She had heard how he got the name Raging Bull and why there had been a long-time feud between him and her people. She could tell that he was an honorable man and that he didn't murder her husband and sons in cold blood.

"Did they die well?" she asked in English.

Both Liam and Azariah nodded. Elk Woman turned to Chief Big Foot and spoke to him at length in their native language. The chief nodded and had some of the warriors take the horses away carrying the bodies of Samuel and his three sons, followed by Elk Woman and her two surviving sons.

The chief then approached Liam and Azariah. "We accept your offer," he said in sign. "We will smoke the pipe of peace."

A few days later, Liam and Azariah returned to their valley near Granite Peak. Sweet Grass and Choke Cherry Woman, who were collecting water, were the first to see their husbands as they rode around the trail behind their cabins and whooped for joy. Before Azariah's feet touched the ground, Sweet Grass was on him like a bear on honey. They embraced and kissed for a long period before their two youngest children, the twins Abigail Little Flower and Solomon White Wolf, tried to get between them so they could get their father's attention.

Choke Cherry Woman waited for Liam to get off his horse and then held out her arms as he approached to give her a long, passionate kiss.

After the happy couple came up for air, Liam paused. "Jason and the children make it back?"

Choke Cherry Woman nodded.

"Speaking of the children," said Azariah, "are they all right?"

"Everyone is fine, husband," said Sweet Grass.

"The question is are you two all right?" said Reverend Hancock as he approached, armed with a rifle. He was followed by Jason, Caleb, Mother and Sister Abigail, Adam Bear Claw, Two Hawks and Clay Basket, White Hawk and Bluebird, along with Spotted Bear and the rest of the children. All were overjoyed by the men's return.

"We were expecting trouble when you two didn't return after the trouble with MacAnnish and his sons," said Jason. "Where did you go?"

"To return the bodies of Samuel MacAnnish and his three sons to the Crow," answered Azariah.

"And make peace with the Crow," said Liam.

Choke Cherry Woman and Sweet Grass' parents were a little surprised. He was the last person they would expect to make peace with his long-time, hated enemy.

"There has been too much bloodshed," said Liam. "I want some relative peace, so we can raise our families without always looking over our shoulders."

"That is the wisest thing I have ever heard you say, husband," said Choke Cherry Woman, beaming with pride.

"Today is a new beginning for us," said Liam "For once, I pray that we can live here in peace."

"Meaning no trouble from the Crow, Da?" asked Luke Medicine Horse.

Liam gently patted his son on his head and smiled. "I sure do hope so, son."

18

A TIME TO LIVE AND A TIME TO DIE

The next few months was a busy time for the Hancock and O'Reilly families. Reverend Hancock, Jason, and Caleb learning how to trap beaver and other fur-bearing animals that would catch a good price at Rendezvous the following summer. Out of all of them, Caleb was the quickest study and caught five beaver his first time out. Reverend Hancock and Jason were better at hunting and reading sign than trapping beaver. They had a hard time getting used to being in freezing water, sometimes waist deep.

The lessons for the younger children hadn't ceased either. Abraham and Jacob were becoming fast learners at riding horses bareback. With the help of Two Hawks, White Hawk, and Adam, they were soon riding horses almost like they were born for it. Caleb was never good at riding bareback, but he kept trying. He and his father finally learned to reload their rifles while riding, which came in handy. When they weren't hunting or trapping, cabins were being built for Azariah's parents, and Jason and Abigail. It took most of the fall to get the two new homes up, but the time winter hit, they were completed.

Spending their first winter in the Rockies in their new home was strange for Jason and Abigail. While they had learned their lessons well from Azariah and Liam and were grateful that the entire family was together, it was still strange compared to how they lived back home in Maryland. Jason did miss his parents and siblings, but he had no regrets uprooting his wife and children and moving west, so they could be near his brother-in-law. He did it all for Abigail and her parents' benefit and she loved him even more for it.

Caleb would visit the O'Reillys' cabin to continue his courtship with Little Fawn and would often go hunting by himself to bring in meat for her family. Liam thought it was unnecessary, but he appreciated the effort. Before long, he welcomed the possibility of a marriage between the two. However, both he and Choke Cherry Woman agreed that they were too young to discuss marriage, despite the fact Caleb had yet to bring it up to them. However, his intentions were to marry Little Fawn eventually, but he wanted to get to know her more and mentioned as much to both his parents and hers, which suited everyone just fine.

When he wasn't courting Little Fawn, Caleb and Adam

would often go hunting or fishing together. The two cousins had become close like brothers and learned a lot from each other as well. While Adam could read and write, there were only two books he had ever read in his life introduced to him by his father—The Holy Bible and Gulliver's Travels by Jonathan Swift. When Caleb and their kin showed up at Rendezvous, they brought with them books by Thomas Paine, Benjamin Franklin and English playwright William Shakespeare. Caleb enjoyed listening to his stepfather read from Shakespeare and reading it himself. He gladly shared the whole book of Shakespeare's plays with Adam, and before long the two cousins were practicing if they were actors on stage. Since Caleb was courting Little Fawn, Adam convinced him to quote or perform for her from his favorite Shakespeare play, Romeo and Juliet.

Liam and Choke Cherry Woman, along with White Hawk and Bluebird, got a good chuckle when Caleb rode up to their cabin one snowy morning quoting the scene when Romeo came to Juliet's window to woo her. Little Fawn thought the effort was cute and she appreciated it, though she had never read Shakespeare. Caleb was a little embarrassed when he found out that she didn't even know who William Shakespeare was nor what his plays were all about. However, she gently lifted his spirits when she asked him if he would teach her the words. Caleb, being over-excited, shouted both a 'yes!' and a 'waugh!'

As for Azariah and his family, there would be a new

member. In the middle of January, a week after celebrating his and his twin sister's birthdays, Sweet Grass announced that she was with child. When she told her husband that morning, he was beside himself at first.

"Are you sure?"

"Of course, I am sure," said Sweet Grass. "We women know these things."

"Yippeeee!"

Reverend and Mother Abigail, along with Jason and Little Abigail and the boys, came running out of their cabins when they heard the commotion. "Is everything all right?" asked Reverend Hancock.

Azariah was dancing in circles with Sweet Grass in his arms. By this time, the rest of the Hancock children came out of their rooms to see what their parents were so happy about. Two Hawks and Clay Basket had also entered the cabin and suspected what was going on.

"Last time he acted like that," said Two Hawks, "my daughter was pregnant with the twins."

Azariah's parents, along with Jason and Abigail, had questioning looks on their faces as if they wanted confirmation.

"It's true," said Azariah. "Mother, Father, Two Hawks and Clay Basket, you're going to have another grandchild!"

The good reverend danced a jig, while Mother and Sister Abigail hugged Sweet Grass. Two Hawks and Clay Basket joined in the hugging, while the Hancock and Allen children joined their Grandpa Hancock in the jig.

After the spring trapping season was over, the two families headed towards the Arapaho summer camp near the Wind River Mountains. Chief Red Hoof had moved the village there at the beginning of spring and managed to avoid any entanglements with the Shoshone. Around May, the Hancock and O'Reilly families arrived and before they got settled in, Azariah and Liam paid their respects to the chief and the council. Two Hawks, who sat on the council, announced that he and Clay Basket would be grandparents again and everyone cheered in celebration. Sweet Grass who was now in the fifth moon of her pregnancy was showing but not by much. With both her mother, mother-in-law and sister-in-law to help her, along with Choke Cherry Woman and Bluebird, there wasn't much to worry about.

Azariah was excited about being a father again, as were his children who could not wait to welcome their new baby brother or sister, even though their mother was not due until September. It was decided among the council that the village would attend the white man's Rendezvous again this summer, which like the previous summer was going to be held at the Green River, or the Siskeedee as it was called. The Hancocks and the O'Reillys would accompany the village, thinking their plews from both the winter and spring trapping seasons would be safer while they were among family and friends.

A few days later, Abraham, Jacob, Sara, Abigail, Solomon, Little Badger and Luke were playing with some of the village children, when two grizzly cubs appeared out of a raspberry bush nearby. Not far behind the cubs was their mother, and she was the opposite of happy. All the children quickly ran for their lives, spreading out in different directions, confusing the enraged she-grizzly. She quickly focused on Luke Medicine Horse O'Reilly who was running to the nearest tree to climb, but he tripped and fell. Before she was on him, though, a gunshot rang out and a musket ball hit her side. It came from Reverend Hancock's Kentucky rifle.

"Run for your life, Luke! Hurry!"

The young boy managed to run to the tree, when the she-grizzly, ignoring the pain in her side, turned her attention back on him, but Reverend Hancock distracted her. "Over here, you oversized flea bag," he shouted. "Come and get me!"

By this time, Azariah, Liam and nearly half a dozen warriors armed with rifles, bows and arrows were ready to take out the beast, but she was already too close to the good reverend, who tried in vain to outrun her.

"Father!" shouted Azariah, but it was too late. The beast was on Reverend Hancock and no one could get a clear shot at her without hitting him.

Wandering Bear suddenly rammed a spear into the side of the grizzly, which caused her to roar, disregarding Reverend Hancock and focusing on the cause of pain in her side. This was the break the men needed, and they opened fire from their rifles, while those who were armed with bows and arrows let loose, turning the she-grizzly into one giant pin cushion. All ammunition found its mark, but the beast, like most of her kind, was extremely hard to kill and would not die without a fight. She roared and grunted as every new arrow was shot into her. Azariah fired his rifle into her, while Liam reloaded and vice versa. Every shot found its mark. The beast was spewing blood from her mouth. Suddenly, she turned back towards the bush and collapsed.

Knowing grizzlies were most dangerous when they were dying, Azariah, Liam and some of the warriors who had rifles reloaded them and cautiously approached the beast before firing a volley of musket balls into her, just to make sure she was dead. When she wasn't moving, everyone was satisfied.

Azariah immediately ran to his father, who was being attended to by Wandering Bear. "How is he?"

The medicine man looked dour. "I speak with a straight tongue, He Who Walks Tall," he said. "It doesn't look good."

It wasn't good from where anyone could see. Reverend Hancock's scalp was ripped off from left to right, but that wasn't the worst of it. The grizzly had slashed deep gashes into his chest and neck area and his right arm was completely mangled, not to mention his right shoulder was dislocated. He was still breathing, but he was unconscious.

Wander Bear's granddaughter, Laughing Bird, who had

become a healer like her grandfather, had Reverend Hancock taken to her tipi, where she and some others would clean his wounds and sew them up before infection took in. However, she agreed with her grandfather. It may all be in vain, but she would try to save the father of He Who Walks Talk, a man who she proudly called her brother.

Reverend Hancock's wounds were worse than everyone feared. The grizzly had broken two of his ribs, which may have punctured a lung. He didn't have long to live. Azariah told his mother, his wife and sister to keep the children out of the tipi. They didn't need to see their grandfather like this.

"No," said Reverend Hancock as he regained consciousness. "I want to see them."

All of Reverend Nehemiah Hancock's grandchildren from oldest to youngest came inside. All of them were crying. He requested Liam O'Reilly's son, Luke, and Howling Wolf's son, Little Badger. "Do not grieve, my little angels," he said. "I can go in peace, knowing that beast didn't harm a hair on any of you or any of the children from the village."

"Don't die, Grandpa," pleaded Jacob. "Please don't die."

"I am afraid I don't have a choice in the matter, Jacob," said Reverend Hancock before he started coughing up some blood. Laughing Bird managed to wipe the blood from his mouth with Mother Abigail's handkerchief. "Know this," he said. "I love each and every one of you, and I am proud to have been your grandfather."

Caleb could not contain himself and left. Jason and

Abigail were about to go after him, but knowing he didn't have long, Reverend Hancock asked them to stay. When he had the grandchildren leave the tipi, he looked into the sad eyes of his children and wife. "My daughter, Abigail, and my son, Azariah," he said. "No father can be prouder of his children than I am of you two. I am a happy man."

Little Abigail broke down in tears, comforted by Jason, with his arms around her. "She will need you now more than ever, Jason," said Reverend Hancock. "Protect her. Love her as I loved her mother."

Jason nodded at his father-in-law. A single tear ran down his cheek. Reverend Hancock quickly turned to his son. Azariah knelt beside his dying father, tears flowing down both cheeks. His father immediately stared at Sweet Grass, who was standing behind Azariah next to Mother Abigail. "Sweet Grass," said Reverend Hancock. "Azariah will need you more than ever. I now know you two were meant to be together. God has foreseen it."

Sweet Grass gently placed her hands on her husband's shoulder as he wept beside his father. Feeling the end nearing, Reverend Hancock stretched out his left arm towards his wife. She knelt beside him as she grabbed it, tears flowing from her eyes. "My dear Abigail," said Reverend Hancock. "You have made me the happiest man in the whole world."

"I thank God every day we have been together," said Mother Abigail. "I pray that I have been worthy of your love."

"No woman has been more worthy of it than you, my

love," responded the reverend before coughing up more blood. "You are the best of wives."

With those words, Reverend Hancock closed his eyes. He continued to cough more blood, before saying his final words. "Father, into Thy hands, I commend my spirit."

19

A NEW DAY

Reverend Nehemiah Hancock was given an Arapaho funeral.
His body was washed and cleansed by Sweet Grass and Clay
Basket. Azariah cut his braided hair, as did Liam and his
family. Sweet Grass and her relatives did the same. Mother
Abigail and Jason asked why they did that. Azariah informed
them that it was a sign of mourning. Many tribes practiced it,
not just the Arapaho.

"Well," said Jason, "me and the boys were in need of a
haircut anyway." Jason cut his hair, as did Caleb, Abraham
and Jacob. Much to their surprise both Mother and Sister
Abigail cut their hair according to tribal customs as well.

The funeral was held early the next morning. The
Hancock patriarch was held up on a funeral scaffold at the
burial ground where many had been buried in the same
manner before him. This was a huge honor, for no white man

or any other outsider had been buried in the village according to tribal customs. Wandering Bear performed the ceremony, burning sage grass and chanting to the Man Above, asking Him to welcome home White Medicine Eagle to the Happy Hunting Grounds. When he was done, Jason was allowed to read from his father-in-law's Bible. He read from Psalms 23:4-6: "Yea, though I walk through the valley of the shadow of death, I will fear no evil: for thou art with me; thy rod and thy staff they comfort me. Thou preparest a table before me in the presence of mine enemies: thou anointest my head with oil; my cup runneth over. Surely goodness and mercy shall follow me all the days of my life: and I will dwell in the house of the Lord forever."

When the funeral was over, Wandering Bear, Laughing Bird and Chief Red Hoof approached Azariah. "Your father was a good man," said Wandering Bear. "He touched many lives here."

"Remember the man he was," added Red Hoof, "how he lived, and take comfort in that."

Azariah nodded his thanks and to all those who came to pay their respects. Reverend Hancock's death hit his family hard, but his daughter and eldest grandson were having the most difficult time. Before Jason had married Abigail, her father was the only male role model Caleb had. Even during the dark times, her father kept the family close and protected, and more importantly, they were happy.

Now, as he lay on the funeral scaffold, Sister Abigail

slowly approached it and fell to her knees, weeping. Jason stood by her, gently placing his loving hands on her shoulder. Caleb, who had been quiet the entire time, couldn't handle losing his grandfather. He was angry, mostly at the grizzly for taking his beloved grandfather from him.

The beast had already been skinned and butchered for food. It was agreed that the claws would be given to Reverend Hanock's family, but Caleb wanted more than that. "Wandering Bear," said Caleb to the medicine man. "I want you to put a curse on that bear, her cubs and all of their kind!"

The medicine man slowly shook his head. "I can't do that."

"You can't or you won't?"

"Caleb!" shouted Jason. "What is the matter with you?"

Wandering Bear raised his hand. "He is angry, as he should be," he said. "But you can't take vengeance or put a curse on an animal."

"Why not?" asked Caleb, raising his voice.

His mother had heard enough. She felt he was out of line, even in his grief, and was about to scold him, when her mother intervened. "Caleb," said Mother Abigail, "if your grandfather was killed by a human, would you want vengeance?"

"Yes!"

"Is that what your grandfather would have wanted?"

Caleb suddenly went silent. He was still angry, but he was calming down when his grandmother approached him. "I loved your grandfather more than anything, more than life itself," she said. "I knew him best, and he would not want any of us to spend one second in vengeance." She gently touched his face before hugging him.

This was more than Azariah could handle, so he went down by the lake to grieve alone. As he sat by a tree, he just cried. "Help me God," he said. "I don't understand." Losing his father, almost a year after being reunited with him, was more painful than Azariah realized, and he continued to weep. Suddenly, he felt a hand on his shoulder and it was none other than Sweet Grass. She was always there for him, no matter what. He lowered his huge head into her bosom as she wrapped her arms around his huge frame. This was not the first time she had comforted him in such a manner, and it would certainly not be the last. It was one of the reasons he loved her so much. She had her ways of making him happy and consoled.

He raised his head a moment and gently placed his hand on her protruding belly. "He would have loved to have seen his grandchild come into the world."

"I know," said Sweet Grass. "Wandering Bear and Red Hoof were right, though."

"About what?" asked Azariah.

"Don't mourn how he died," said Sweet Grass. "But take comfort in how he lived."

Azariah thought about that for a moment. He always remembered and cherished the good times he had with his father. Even though the reunion was short-lived following a sixteen-year separation, he couldn't think of one bad memory of his father, even if he tried.

"A new day is coming, husband," said Sweet Grass. "Like all things, we must go on live it."

"Since when did you get so wise?" asked Azariah.

Sweet Grass just shrugged as her husband smiled for the first time. They sat there together in the shade for a while before returning to the village. It was a new day, and life must go on.

EPILOGUE

After selling their plews at Rendezvous and re-outfitting themselves for another year, Azariah and Liam and their families decided that they were going to winter with their Arapaho and Cheyenne relatives. Some Cheyenne villages, including that of Black Cloud, went south to visit and winter at Bent's Fort to trade. Liam and Choke Cherry Woman were taking the children to Bent's Fort to be with their Cheyenne kin, plus it would be the first time they had ever taken a trip there.

Azariah and Liam had met William Bent and his brother, Charles, nine years ago at the 1828 Rendezvous, when the former was putting plans in place to create his now-famous fort. Azariah and Sweet Grass had both been meaning to visit the fort, but never got around to it, and with Sweet Grass in her current condition, it was not a good time to go.

They said their goodbyes to the O'Reillys and agreed to meet them in the spring for the spring trapping season. It was the middle of September and Sweet Grass had gone into labor. As with her four previous pregnancies, she was in a tipi surrounded by her mother, sister-in-law Prairie Bird Woman, and the medicine woman, Laughing Bird. This time, both Mother and Sister Abigail were with her as well to help with the delivery in any way they could, while the men waited outside.

As he was with the births of all his children, Azariah Hancock was a nervous wreck, driving everyone crazy.

"Jesus, Azariah, calm down," said Jason. "It's your wife who is having the baby, yet you're making me nervous."

"He is always like this when sister is with child," laughed Howling Wolf.

"I'm glad I wasn't like this when his sister gave birth to my children," responded Jason.

Azariah ignored them while continuing to pace back and forth. Finally, Two Hawks invited him to sit. "If I told you once, I have told you a thousand times," he said, "women have been having babies since time immemorial. Leave the worries to them."

Heeding his father-in-law's advice and finally sitting, Azariah was still fidgeting when suddenly a baby cried from inside the tipi. Azariah bolted off the log that he and Two Hawks were sitting on and almost ran into his mother.

"I have a new grandson!" she shouted in Arapaho. Both

she and her daughter had been learning the language better than Jason who was still struggling but managed to at least have a conversation in the Arapaho tongue.

"Sweet Grass," said Azariah. "Is she well?"

"She is fine, son," answered his mother. "Go and see her."

"Come, children," said Azariah as he entered the tipi, followed by his four older children who were excited to welcome their new baby brother into the world. Sweet Grass sat there as she breastfed her new son. Azariah knelt beside her and kissed her cheek. Then he gently stroked the soft hair of their new son. Like his siblings, he could pass for a full-blooded Arapaho. The difference was he had their father's red hair. Like his brother, Adam, and sister, Abigail, he also had their father's blue eyes.

"He looks like Grandpa," said five-year-old Solomon White Wolf.

"Which one?" asked Azariah. "Grandpa Two Hawks or Grandpa Hancock?"

"Both."

"I agree," said Caleb. "He does look like both of his grand-fathers."

Azariah and Sweet Grass looked at each other, reading each other's minds. "Then it is settled," said Azariah. "His name shall be Nehemiah Two Hawks Hancock."

"It is a good name," said Two Hawks, beaming with pride.

"Of course, you would think that it is a good name," joked Clay Basket.

Sweet Grass gave the baby to his father. As Azariah held his new son, he presented him to both his grandparents. Mother Abigail gently took the baby as tears of joy flowed down her cheeks. As she stood next to Two Hawks and Clay Basket, she raised her head and said, "Thank you, God. Thank you, thank you!"

ACKNOWLEDGMENTS

First and foremost, I want to thank Jesus for giving me the talent to daydream and to write, and for allowing me to put my dreams into novels. To my entire family and friends, from my parents to my cousins, and all my friends from Montana to Maryland for their undying love and support. To four of the greatest Western authors, whose shoelaces I am unworthy to tie, Win Blevins, David Robbins, Lane R. Warenski and John Legg, not just for your novels that I have read, but the advice and knowledge about an almost long-forgotten era in our American History that you have given me has been extremely valuable. To Candy Felicia and Ryon Sun Rhodes for the valuable information on the history of the Cheyenne and Arapaho Nations as well as pointing me in the right direction on how to write my stories from a Native point of view. And last but not least, a big thank you to Nick Wale, Kat Turner, Cathy Jones and the entire DS Productions crew for editing, publishing and promoting my stories and getting them out there. I am forever in your debt. Aho!!

Made in the USA
Las Vegas, NV
25 February 2022

44608165R10089